W9-BRG-707

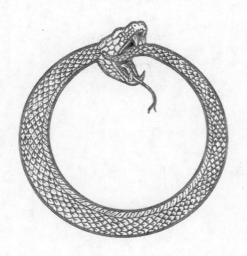

Books by Aden Polydoros
available from Inkyard Press

Middle Grade

Ring of Solomon

Young Adult

The City Beautiful
Bone Weaver

RING OF SOLOMON

ADEN POLYDOROS

inkyard PRESS

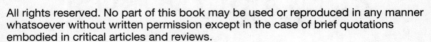

Dedicated to all the kids who are still waiting for their enchanted cupboard, haunted house, or magic-school admission letter.

NAOMI WAS GONE.

One second, she was there, smack-dab in the middle of San Pancras's downtown flea market, wearing her huge pink sunglasses and the baseball cap Mom had bought her at Disneyland last summer. And then I turned around just for a moment. By the time I looked back, she had vanished into the swarm of bargain hunters and chattering tourists.

My stomach dropped. No, no, no. Mom was going to kill me.

"Naomi?" I pushed past a man haggling over an overpriced snow globe. By sheer luck, I avoided crashing into a vendor selling plates and bowls. Considering how ugly the dishes were, breaking them would've been an act of mercy.

I swiveled around, searching for Naomi in the crowd, which was so densely packed that it wiggled down the street like a blob of Jell-O. She wasn't crouched over the battalion of stuffed animals and action figures lined up on one man's carpet. She wasn't tossing her empty soda bottle into the trash can or scraping gum off the bottom of her flip-flops.

"Naomi?" My voice cracked like an old record. It had been doing that a lot lately, ever since I turned twelve, but it wasn't just puberty this time. My throat tightened in panic. "Naomi?! This isn't funny."

A hand yanked on my sleeve. I turned, not knowing how nervous I'd been until I swallowed and felt my lips tremble. There Naomi was, just standing there with her stupid sunglasses and Minnie Mouse cap, her blond hair poking up in random directions. She inherited Mom's upturned nose and serious eyes, but her dimpled chin and goofy smile were all Dad's.

"Where were you, you dolt?" I asked as she slurped down the rest of her Coke. "I told you not to wander off."

She grinned. "Zach, you have to come see this. I found the perfect thing. Mom's gonna love it."

Naomi pulled me down the rows of vendors. The sun beat down on us, the air ripe with the smells of pizza grease and coconut-scented sunscreen. All I wanted was to go back home and play video games, but Mom's birthday was this Monday. Turning forty seemed like it deserved something special. Roses and drawings wouldn't cut it this time.

Every month, Mom would drive nearly an hour up to San Francisco to drag us to the famous Alameda flea market. Next to it, the San Pancras swap meet was a cheaper knockoff than the plasticky purses a pink-haired woman was hollering were real Gucci. There were only three things our coastal town was known for—its quiet streets lined with Spanish mission–style houses, the abandoned cement factory at its outskirts, and having a name that sounded suspiciously like a human organ.

Naomi led me to an old man stooped in front of a card table heaped with musty paperbacks, brass vases, and picture frames. There was so much stuff, I expected the table legs to collapse at any moment, drowning everything within five feet in a tsunami of junk. The fire department would have to dig us out.

"Naomi." I looked at her. What did she expect to find here, except for rat droppings and mothballs?

"One second. It's right around here somewhere." Eyes sparkling in excitement, she dug through the tangle of jewelry sitting in a glass ashtray. Mostly just Mardi Gras beads, plastic bangles, and brooches so gaudy even our mom would turn her nose up at them. Naomi fished a ring from the bottom of the pile and showed it to me.

It was a thick golden signet ring. The circular panel on top was engraved with a six-pointed Star of David and surrounded by crimson stones. Garnets maybe, but probably just glass. Hebrew letters encircled the band, though for all I knew, they could've been an advertisement for Burger King.

I tried the ring on my finger, but it slipped right off. "Naomi, it's going to be too big for her. It's a guy's ring."

"But don't you think she'd love it?"

Mom went a little crazy when it came to Jewish stuff, even though she was about as religious as a bacon cheeseburger. She collected menorahs and dreidels, Yiddish pamphlets and Hebrew books none of us could read, corny old paintings of wizard-bearded rabbis and clarinet-playing klezmer musicians, and more. An entire corner of the kitchen was devoted to her hoard, but over the years, the stuff had overflowed into the rest of our home as well. Somehow, one of her weird oil paintings had ended up in my bedroom. You think *Nosferatu* or *Frankenstein* is bad? Try falling asleep beneath the bearded scowls of an entire room of Torah scholars. That's what I'd call nightmare fuel.

I turned the ring around in my hand. The sunlight danced across the red gemstones. Big, gaudy, and very Jewish. Mom would go totally nuts over it.

"Come on, Zach," Naomi said, tugging on my sleeve. "Come *on*. It's perfect."

Sighing, I held up the ring. "Excuse me, how much is this?"

The old man leaned over the table, squinting past his half-moon glasses. He smacked his lips. "Twenty dollars!"

Twenty dollars? Talk about a rip-off. We could buy Mom a ring from Kohl's or an entire box of fancy chocolates for that much.

I didn't want to haggle, even though people haggled at flea markets all the time. Haggling would feel like leaning down to pick up dropped change, and I'd stopped doing that since Jeffrey Cooper in history class threw pennies at me. I knew there was nothing wrong with it, but just the thought made me cringe in embarrassment.

I turned. "Naomi, it's too…"

She had her lower lip jutted out and was giving me the kind of puppy-eyed look that was basically kryptonite for big brothers. A shiver of dread passed through me. If I left now, the tears would start, and then the screaming. Trust me, her tantrum would make World War III look like a schoolyard fight, no joke.

"Zach, you have *thirty* dollars," Naomi said.

"Yeah, but there's the field trip to the zoo on Monday, and I want to have enough for the gift shop." But it was more than that. I knew that Dominic Bianchi would be there, and since we were in the same homeroom, maybe we'd end up in the gift shop at the same time. I could see it in my head—he'd be walking down the aisle, running his fingers over the shelves' contents, looking longingly at a souvenir or two. He really liked wolves, so maybe he'd be eyeing a T-shirt or poster in the car-nivore section. And I would come up, money already in hand, and buy it for him.

"Zach, please." Naomi begged at me with her eyes. "Mom will love it."

Reluctantly, I counted out the crumpled bills. Five, ten, twenty. I only got ten dollars a month for allowance and two-fifty to play with our neighbors' cat, Mags, when they were away on business. Oh well, there probably wasn't anything in-teresting at the gift shop, and it wasn't like Dominic would even notice me. Why would he? We weren't friends, even though I wished we could be.

"Here," I muttered, handing the money to the man.

He pocketed the bills. "Smart choice, kid."

"Is it an antique?" I asked, already regretting my life choices.

"Who knows."

"Where'd you get it?"

"It was in a fish."

"A fish," I repeated stupidly.

He nodded. "A sea bass. When I cut it open to cook it, the ring was buried inside its stomach. Those bass, they'll eat anything."

"Really?" A small smile touched my lips. Talk about a wicked origin story.

"Ew, that's so nasty," Naomi said as we walked back to the flea market's entrance, where we had promised to meet Mom and Dad at noon. She made a face. "Let's not tell Mom."

For once, I agreed with her.

2

"I CAN'T BELIEVE we're doing this," I muttered, propping my foot against the back of the driver's seat. A blur of blue ocean and beachfront houses rippled past the window. "Do I really have to go, Dad? Can't we just go to the beach instead?"

"It's too late to complain now, kiddo. You're stuck." He grinned and met my eye in the rearview mirror. "Remember, you used to love going to Grandma's."

"Yeah, like when I was ten. I'm almost thirteen now, Dad."

"Don't remind me." He rolled his eyes. "Besides, I don't hear you complaining at Christmastime."

That was because Grandma gave the best presents. I was pretty sure it was her way of trying to convert us, like if she showered me and Naomi with enough stuff, we'd go over to Team Jesus.

"It's not even a holiday," I said in annoyance. "Why have a barbeque in the middle of the month, for no reason?"

"Because she wants to show off the new tile," Dad said.

I groaned. "That's even worse."

He arched an eyebrow. "Oh? So, you'd rather be moping at home now?"

"I'd rather be playing video games with Sandra than spend my Saturday stuck listening to Grandma brag about her *floor.*"

"Zach loves Sandra, Zach loves Sandra," Naomi sang, knocking her head against my shoulder.

"Shut up, gnome." I shoved her lightly in the arm. My cheeks burned, and I was pretty sure if I glanced in the mirror, my face would be redder than a fire hydrant. "We're just friends."

"A crush is nothing to be ashamed of, sport," Dad said with a laugh.

"It's not a crush!"

Mom looked back and gave me a smile, an almost reassuring one. Sometimes, I wondered if she knew the truth. If she could tell.

I reached into my pocket for the ring I'd bought at the swap meet, just to make sure it was still there. The more I thought about it, the more I worried it was a piece of junk.

Grandma and Grandpa lived in the fancy part of San Pancras, where people were so snobby that even their dogs seemed to sneer down at us. Our grandparents' chunky white house overlooked the beachfront. Mom said the style was midcentury modern, whatever that meant. To me, it looked like a pile of Legos with windows. If I were a millionaire, I'd build a castle for myself, complete with a moat and drawbridge.

There were already several cars parked in the driveway. We

found a spot at the end of the line. Our station wagon looked so lame next to my grandpa's fancy-schmancy Porsche and my uncle's huge Hummer.

Dad ran his fingers over the Porsche's glossy paint job as we walked past it. He sighed. "This is why I shouldn't have gone to art school."

"Then you wouldn't have met Mom," Naomi said, because like me, she had heard the story about our parents' first date a gazillion times.

"Tuck your shirt in," Mom told me, ringing the doorbell. "And Naomi, stop chewing on your hair."

"Sorry," Naomi said through a mouthful of her ponytail. Her hair was as light and wispy as corn silk, just like our dad's, whereas mine took after our mom's—brown, wild, and the sworn enemy of hairdressers. I was pretty sure that my cowlicks alone defied at least three laws of gravity and physics.

The door opened and our grandma waltzed out like a star on the red carpet. She wore a sparkly silver dress and had her blond hair done up in a fancy do that kinda made it seem like she was wearing a beehive.

"Oh, Peter, it's so good to see you!" Grandma cooed, hugging my dad. "And Emily. Stunning as always, dear."

Mom smiled stiffly as Grandma leaned in to kiss her cheek, looking like she'd much rather lock lips with a fish. Ever since Grandma had told Mom that she wanted Naomi to get baptized, things had gone nuclear between the two of them. When it happened, I remembered how back in preschool or kindergarten, Grandma had taken me somewhere where a strange

15

man had sprinkled water on my head. I was a little worried that I actually *was* baptized, and what that really meant, and if I was Jewish still or not.

Sometimes, I didn't feel Jewish enough, no matter how many menorahs and seder plates Mom managed to cram in her china cabinet. We only went to temple for the big holidays like Rosh Hashanah and Yom Kippur, and if you got between Naomi and her bacon, she'd go rabid. I would know—a few months ago, Naomi had nearly bitten off my thumb when I tried stealing half of her Bacon 'N Egg McMuffin.

Of course, Jeffrey didn't care whether I felt Jewish enough or not when he started bullying me. At first it was the penny thing. Then he'd knocked off my baseball cap at recess and asked me where my horns were. I wished I could stand up to him, except he had an entire gang of friends, while I just had Sandra. No doubt, my best friend could throw a mean right hook, but I wasn't about to test my luck against Team Neanderthal.

Once Grandma finished smothering Naomi in hugs and kisses, she turned to me. Twelve was way too old to be hugged, but I toughed it out anyway, and groaned inwardly as she kissed me on the forehead. I hoped she hadn't left a mark.

Dad clapped a hand over my shoulder. "Mom, you're embarrassing him."

"A grandson shouldn't be embarrassed to hug his grandmother." She pulled back to study me and Naomi closely. She always had to do this. No matter the occasion, she'd complain about something. Maybe it would be the length of my hair, or the style of my clothes, or how a girl Naomi's age should be wearing dresses instead of shorts. It was an honored family tradition for her. This time she just plucked a piece of lint from my shirt, clucked her tongue, and gave my mom a long look. "Wrinkles. You really must do a better job of ironing their clothes, Emily."

Mom's eyebrow twitched. She looked half-tempted to turn this beach party into a bloodbath. "Not all of us can afford to pay people to wash our clothing, Catherine."

"Shame." She swiveled around and strode inside. As soon as her back was turned, I rubbed at the greasy patch her lipstick had left on my forehead.

Dad sighed, herding us into the house.

We hadn't been here since last Christmas. The silver globes and gold snowflakes hanging from the staircase railing and shelves had been replaced by pink roses and cut crystal. Naomi raced to the bowls of pink-and-white M&M's on the snack table, but I held back, itchy with the feeling of being watched. My fingers strayed to my pocket, tracing the ring's worn engravings.

"Hey, kid, get me a hotdog!" a raspy voice said from behind me.

I swiveled around, drawing my breath in sharply. The hallway was deserted except for my grandparents' Afghan hound, Clarence. With the dog's long flaxen hair, he looked, well, a lot like Grandma. Give him a beehive, and they'd practically be twins.

I chuckled nervously. I had probably just imagined the voice, even if it did look like Clarence's mouth had moved.

Clarence nudged me with his snout. "Oh, come on, kid. Do you know how gross kibble is?"

My jaw dropped. No way.

"Naomi, did you hear...?" I looked over my shoulder, but she had already followed the grown-ups out to the patio. As Clarence settled on the shiny new marble floor with a heaving sigh, I squatted down next to him.

He rolled his deep brown eyes up at me. "Well, kid? You keep your mouth open like that any longer, a bug's gonna fly in."

"Am I asleep?" I whispered. "Or dead?"

"If you were dead, do you really think you'd be here?" he asked, giving a weary look around us.

Well, to be fair, being trapped at snobby family get-togethers was the closest thing to hell on earth, next to fourth period with Jeffrey.

"Since when did you learn to talk?" I asked. "Can all dogs do that?"

"Hotdog first, kid. Then you can ask all the questions you want."

I went out to the patio, feeling kind of dreamy. Maybe I was asleep after all.

Along with Grandma and Grandpa, there was my aunt and uncle, and my teenage cousin, Samantha. Samantha was basically the superstar of the family—head of the drama club, an all-expenses-paid scholarship to Otis College of Art and Design next year, Instagram influencer, yada yada yada. Every time we had a barbeque or holiday dinner, my aunt and uncle boasted about her accomplishments, and all I could say was that I'd scored a C on my math test or had a very impressive bowel movement.

"Here comes the man of the hour!" Grandpa said as I walked over. He pulled that same line every other visit, and I still had no idea what it meant. It sounded like something he'd stolen from a TV commercial.

"Is there anything wrong with Clarence?" I asked.

He arched his bushy eyebrows. "Wrong how?"

"His, uh, bark just sounds a little different."

"The dog's getting old, Zach."

I was pretty sure old age didn't cause dogs to magically begin talking, but what did I know? Shrugging, I snagged a hotdog from the stack beside the grill.

"Hey, hold your horses," Dad said with a startled laugh. "Those are still cold."

"I'll survive." I took a big bite to prove it.

Naomi paused in the middle of nomming on her burger to make a face. "You're so gross."

"Says the one with ketchup all over her chin." I hurried away before Mom and Grandma could get in another argument over our manners and how we were being raised.

Naomi followed after me. "Why'd you do that?"

"What? You've never tried a cold hotdog before. You're missing out." I pretended to take another bite. "Delicious."

She groaned. "Stop it. You're going to make me puke."

We went back into the den, where Clarence was curled up by the snacks table. He lifted his head as we entered.

"You've got to see this," I told Naomi, before dangling the hotdog over the dog's head. "Say something, Clarence."

He wagged his tail and barked. Barked. A perfectly normal sound.

What the…? I was sure I hadn't imagined it.

"Clarence, I know you can speak."

"Zach, cut it out," Naomi said in exasperation.

"No, he was actually talking to me just a few minutes ago." My cheeks prickled with heat. Clarence bumped his snout against my leg, and I tossed the hotdog to him. Once he scarfed it down, he nudged me a second time. Inside my pocket, the ring pressed against my thigh.

The ring.

I reached into my pocket and snared the band in my fingers, its metal hot against my palm.

"Thanks for the chow, kid," Clarence said, licking his chops. "But you really ought to have given me a warm one, you know? Cold hotdogs are almost as bad as stale kibble, and let me tell you, I wouldn't wish that upon my worst enemy."

"See," I said breathlessly to Naomi. "I told you. He's talking."

Naomi rolled her eyes. "I'm not five anymore, you know. This isn't funny."

I took the ring from my pocket and pressed it into her hand, twining fingers with her so the band touched both our palms. "Clarence, say something else. Tell us what you think of Grandpa."

"That cranky old man?" Clarence puffed air through his teeth. "He tells me I shouldn't chase squirrels, but you know what I think? I think he just wishes he could chase them himself!"

Naomi gasped. My shoulders loosened at the sight of the shock blazing across her features.

"Zach, it's a magic ring," she whispered.

I rolled my eyes. No duh.

"What about Grandma?" I asked Clarence. "What do you think of her?"

Clarence leveled his chin and flipped his luscious locks out of his eyes. "My fur's way better."

I wasn't about to argue with that one.

"Do you know more about this ring?" I asked the dog, but he had already turned his attention to grooming himself. I sighed and followed Naomi back outside.

No surprise—the adults were arguing about sports or the president or something. Samantha sprawled on the patio chair, typing furiously into her phone. She barely even glanced at us as we neared.

Naomi took two steps toward the gathering. "Mom! Mom! Look at—"

I snagged her shoulder before she could say more and shook my head. If this ring *was* magical, telling Mom and Dad would ruin it. It had been hard enough convincing them to let me go to Sandra's paintball party this year. They'd been sure I'd shoot my eye out with a paintball or get hit by an exploding CO_2 tank. Knowing how uptight they got about our safety, if they knew the ring could make people understand animals, they'd probably think Naomi and I would use it to befriend mountain lions or great white sharks!

Come to think of it, that wasn't such a bad idea. Jeffrey

bragged all the time about going out on his dad's boat and how his family belonged to the San Pancras Yacht Club. If I could convince a shark—or even just a mean-looking dolphin—to pop out at him, he'd totally have to buy himself a new set of swim trunks. Bonus points if it happened in front of his friends.

"Naomi and I are going down to the beach," I called to Mom. She waved me on. Once we made it out of sight, I stopped Naomi. "Listen, I'll get Mom another birthday gift, but not this. This is my ring. I paid for it."

"But I found it!" she protested.

"No offense, Naomi, but you're nine. I'll let you use it with my supervision." A part of me wished I hadn't told her at all. "We need to keep this a secret, okay? Just the two of us. You can't go around blabbing to your friends or your teachers at school. No one, got it?"

The last thing I needed was for the ring to fall into the wrong hands. As in, Jeffrey's hands. With the entire animal kingdom at his mercy, he'd turn my life into a nightmare.

"I won't tell anyone," Naomi swore.

"Promise."

She held out her pinkie. I hooked mine around hers. It had been a few years since I'd believed in the absolute power of pinkie promises—or any promises, really—but it would have to do this time.

"Why are we going over here?" she asked as we trudged through knee-high patches of yellowed grass. A cool mist brushed off the ocean, leaving the air tangy with the scent of sea brine.

"Don't you want to try talking to fish?"

She pointed at a seagull. "What about birds?"

I took out the ring and linked hands with her. "Try calling it."

"Hey, Mr. Bird!"

The seagull continued its slow, lazy loop overhead, joined by several others.

Naomi frowned. "It's not working."

An idea came to me. "Tell it we have food."

"Hey, Mr. Gull! We have chips for you."

The seagull landed on the beach at our feet.

"Chips. Chips. Chips." Its beak opened and closed. All of a sudden, I didn't like the look in its beady white eyes. "Chips. Chips."

"Uh-oh." Naomi pointed upward.

More seagulls had begun to swarm, soon joined by a handful of sandpipers and blackbirds. Their shrieks and chitters merged into a roar as creepy as the rumbling of thunder:

"Chipschipschipschipschipschipschipschipschipschipschipschips chips."

I exchanged a look with Naomi. The wonder in her face had faded into pale, trembling fear.

"I don't think we have enough chips," she whispered.

"Yeah? No kidding!" I flinched as a seagull swooped down, coming close enough that I felt its talons cut the air above my head. I wondered if seagulls ate meat, and then decided I really didn't want to find out. "Come on, let's go!"

Naomi cried out as a seagull dived toward her. I gripped her hand tightly in mine, and we raced across the dunes. Birds surrounded us in a screaming white flurry. Gagging on the smell of dusty feathers and bird dung, I shielded my eyes with my hand.

"Duck your head down," I shouted to Naomi. "Protect your eyes."

We ran for the line of shrubs bordering our grandparents' property. A gull twisted its claws in my hair. Naomi's sweaty hand slipped from mine like a wet bar of soap. I lost my balance, tumbled forward, fell, scraping my knees on the sand and sawgrass.

Being eaten by seagulls wasn't exactly how I planned to go. As far as untimely deaths were concerned, it would only be slightly less humiliating than being squashed by a clown car.

I hopped the small picket fence separating the backyard from the shoreline and helped Naomi over to the other side. Ahead, the adults watched us approach in stunned silence, the hotdogs and burgers smoking on the grill. My cousin Samantha whipped out her phone, crowing something about TikTok or Instagram.

My mom was the first one to leap into action. She ran toward us, shouting for us to go inside, go inside now. She scooped Naomi up in her arms, and moments later, I felt Dad's hand close around my upper arm. He drew me against himself, dragged me forward, guarding my body with his own.

Overhead, the birds screamed bloody murder.

3

FROM THE SAFETY of the den, we watched the birds raid our dinner. Entire bowls of chips vanished in the blink of an eye. Hotdogs were snatched from the grill, still smoking, and carried off in all their greasy glory. Even the brownies and apple pie became the birds' pirate booty, which was probably a good thing. Grandma's "famous" brownies tasted like chocolate chalk, and that was being generous.

"This is *totally* going to go viral," Samantha said, taking selfies against the ceiling-length window's backdrop. Already, nasty lumps of white gull poop covered the pavestones. "Goodbye, Kim Kardashian. Hello, Samantha Darlington."

"Not my zinnias!" Grandma exclaimed in horror as the remaining seagulls began mauling the garden. Samantha must have considered Grandma's reaction meme-worthy, because she started filming again.

"What did you do, Zachary?" Dad demanded. Oh man, he'd brought out my full name. Not good.

"I didn't do anything, Dad, I swear." I pushed my hair out of my face and grimaced as I touched a wet spot. Ugh. Note to self: never underestimate the vengeance of hungry seagulls.

"Zach has a magic ring!" Naomi announced. I shot her an ugly look, but she kept on blabbing. "He can talk to animals with it. He told the birds we had chips."

Dad chuckled sarcastically. "Is that so?"

I rolled my eyes. So much for the sacredness of pinkie promises. She couldn't even keep her word for fifteen minutes.

"Tell your daughter this isn't funny," Grandma snapped at my mom, her face growing almost as red as the checkered tablecloth.

I racked my brain for something to say. Now that I knew the ring's power, there was no way I'd let Mom and Dad take it away. At least not before getting payback on Jeffrey or impressing Dominic.

"I threw a hotdog at one," I said quickly. "I'm sorry. I didn't think it'd go berserk like that."

Everyone looked at me: my grandparents with anger, Samantha with her mouth cocked in disgust, Mom and Dad with disappointment.

My mom took a deep breath. "Zachary, you're—"

I sighed. "Grounded. Yeah, I know."

No video games, no computer, no TV. I threw myself down on my bed and stared at the ceiling. Strung on fishing line, painted models drifted in the draft from the open window—a Mothman cryptid, the USCSS *Nostromo* from the 1979 movie *Alien*, the spaceship from *Predator*.

Some boys collected cars or sports stuff. Me? I preferred old monster movies, the real scary kind. Or at least the ones Mom and Dad let me see. My bookshelf was crowded with limited-edition action figures of Frankenstein, Dracula, and the others, crammed up next to yard-sale *Goosebumps* books, and horror comics. On my desk sat a 1:87 scale replica of the *Addams Family* mansion. The crown jewels of my collection were displayed on a shelf Dad built above my desk: rare, fully illustrated hardcovers of all the old classics.

Monster movies were kind of a big tradition in our house. My dad and I watched them all the time. We went to the local theater every month for their old-school horror special. At first, it was *Beetlejuice* and *Gremlins*, but then last year, he began letting me watch the scarier ones like *The Blob*.

But that was only part of it. The real reason I liked monsters so much was because deep down, I kind of felt like one. Yeah, I couldn't sprout fangs or transform into a wolf, but the thing about monsters was that nobody understood them, and sometimes people just hated them for who they were. So, if they wanted to fit in, they had to file down their teeth and invest in a dog grooming kit, keep their head down, and just stay hidden. And every day, I felt the same.

My phone buzzed in my back pocket. Dad had locked all the game apps somehow, but I still got tweets and text messages.

SANDRA: Is this you??

She had sent me a video. With dread already building in my heart, I clicked on the play button.

Samantha must have started filming even before Naomi and I had tumbled past the trees. The sixty-second video showed us running across the lawn, being chased by a tornado of shrieking, chips-obsessed birds. You could even see the moment a seagull pegged me with its perfectly aimed poop-bomb.

"No. No. No." Quickly, I typed out a response.

ZACH: Did my cousin Samantha send it to you?

SANDRA: Lol you kidding? It's got 50k views on TikTok and counting.

"Seriously?" I muttered. When I'd dreamed of going viral, this wasn't what I meant!

I logged on to YouTube and went to Samantha's channel, where she cross-posted her fashion design and drama class videos from TikTok and Instagram. There she had posted the full video, along with a two-minute short showing Grandma's meltdown at the carnage and another of my parents chewing me out over trying to feed the seagulls.

SANDRA: Was it really just a hotdog?

ZACH: No.

SANDRA: Then what did you do to make them so upset?

ZACH: Come over tomorrow. I'll show you.

As I waited for her to respond, a Twitter notification popped up on my phone. Someone had made a GIF showing me getting pummeled with gull poop and sent it as a DM, along with the words BIRD BRAIN!!!

I groaned. Great. The video must have already found its way into Jeffrey's grubby little hands. I dropped my phone onto the bed and took the ring from my pocket, holding it up to the glow of the streetlamp outside.

"What else can you do?" I mused.

No response. Then again, I hadn't really expected one.

"I wish for a new laptop. Get me a new laptop."

I waited a couple minutes, but no laptop appeared from thin air. All right, so it couldn't grant wishes.

"Fire." Sitting up, I flicked my hand toward the window.

Nothing.

"Abracadabra."

No luck.

"I'm guessing there isn't a genie in there?" I asked the ring, shaking it gently. "Someone who can teach Jeffrey and his friends a real lesson? If there is, it'd be really nice if you could show up."

The ring grew hot against my skin, warming my palm like the time I sat too close to the campfire. I held my breath. Slowly, the heat faded.

I waited a minute. Then another.

Sighing in defeat, I collapsed onto my back and closed my eyes. Maybe I could convince a pack of coyotes to chase Jeffrey or bribe some seagulls to pelt him with poop. That would show him.

"You called for me?" a smooth voice said.

My eyes flew open. I lurched into a sitting position with a cry, searching the darkened room. Overhead, the models swung in lazy circles, casting their shadows across the walls. Movement shifted in the corner of my vision. I swiveled around.

A figure sat atop the windowsill, backlit by the red streetlight. His form was immersed in darkness. As he jumped onto the bedroom floor, I caught a glimpse of spread wings, feathers as black and glossy as spilled ink.

"Wh-what…" My lips trembled so hard I couldn't even get the words out. I thought I might scream the way people did in horror movies, but it was like my voice had thickened to maple syrup in my throat. "Are you the guardian of the ring?"

Slowly, he eased to his full height. His wings ruffled and furled against his body, so long they nearly dragged across the floor. He wore a black tunic trimmed with gold thread around the hem and clasped with a jeweled metal sash.

A boy. It was a boy who didn't look much older than me, his hair framing his face in a dark tangle. His gold eyes glowed in the moonlight. He wore a crown whose sharp tines curled like flames, and upon his wrist, a wide golden bracelet studded with garnets.

He would've been pretty, if he weren't so terrifying.

As he stepped forward, the robe parted around his ankles, exposing the taloned feet of a bird of prey. Oh crap, was this my punishment for lying to the seagulls that I'd give them chips? Being cursed by some bird prince?

"Wh-what are you?" I whispered.

"Ashmedai." He smiled, revealing teeth far sharper than those of any human. "King of demons."

4

KING OF DEMONS? I gulped hard. Just my luck. That made a prince of seagulls seem about as menacing as a cat-obsessed granny.

"You don't look like a king," I said weakly, which was probably the stupidest thing I could've said.

His eyes flashed. "You dare question my birthright, human?"

"No! No." I clambered off my bed to put the piece of furniture between us. Not that it would do much good, seeing as he could simply fly over it. "I just mean, aren't kings supposed to be old?"

"I am older than the earth's creation," he declared.

"Well, you look very…well preserved," I said. Scratch that— *this* was the stupidest thing I could've said.

Ashmedai eyed me warily, as if he didn't quite know what to make of me. Most likely, he was watching my estimated IQ plummet by the second.

"Where am I?" he asked at last.

"California. It's in the United States, which is in North America."

"United States," he echoed softly, his gaze clouding over like the name had brought back memories. "The Golden Land…"

"Er, I guess?"

"That was what this ring's previous owner called it," Ash said. "The last time I was awake. Tell me, which century is this?"

"Uh, the twenty-first?"

"No, that can't be right." He shook his head. "That was before the reign of Solomon."

A light bulb flashed in my head. This was a Jewish ring, so maybe… I fished my phone out from beneath the pillow. "Siri, what century is it in the Hebrew calendar?"

"The fifty-eighth century," Siri said. Wow, that was a lot of centuries.

"What is that?" Ashmedai demanded. "Who do you have trapped in that box, human?"

"No one," I said quickly, backing away as he took a step toward me. "It's just a phone, and Siri isn't even a real person. She's a robot."

"Robot," he repeated, confusion shadowing his face. He looked around at the movie posters plastered to the walls, his expression so disoriented that I was a little afraid he had hit his head on the way down to earth and scrambled his brains like a breakfast at IHOP. Or maybe after a few gazillion years, he'd started to go senile. As he was about to say more, there was a knock on the door.

"Zach, don't tell me you're playing video games!" my mom

said in annoyance, knocking once more. "Grounded means grounded."

I cast a hasty look in Ashmedai's direction. Demon kings were scary enough, but angry moms? Those were downright terrifying.

"Hide," I whispered frantically as the knob began to turn. I rushed to the door and caught it just as it swung open, blocking the opening with my body. Peeking my head out, I offered my mom a shaky smile. "Hey, Mom, sorry, I was just video chatting with Sandra."

She looked unconvinced. Frowning, she craned her head over my shoulder and peered into the dark room. I held my breath. There was enough light coming from the street that I knew if she squinted, she'd be able to see Ashmedai.

Feathers rustled softly deeper in. I held my breath, feeling my smile crack by the moment. *Please, please don't let her notice.*

"You're going to have to give me your phone until tomorrow," she said at last, once she decided I wasn't hiding any dirty little secrets. "And go to sleep. It's getting late."

After I pretended to end the make-believe video call, I reluctantly forked over my phone. I waited for her to turn away before closing the door. When I could no longer hear her footsteps, I twisted the lock and leaned against the pane. Apparently, Ashmedai didn't know the meaning of the word *hide*, since he still stood by the bed, examining the action figures lined up along the shelf. He picked up the one of Frankenstein and turned it around in his hands.

"That's not a person either," I added, in case he was wondering if I had shrunk down the monster with the same magic I had used to trap Siri in a smartphone.

Ashmedai must have pressed the action figure's button by mistake, because suddenly creepy music played from the speaker on the figure's back, and the light bulb eyes flashed green. In a mechanical voice, it declared, *"If I cannot inspire love, I will cause fear!"*

Ashmedai drew in a sharp breath. "A golem."

Balanced on our china cabinet was a tiny ceramic replica of a golem, a creature made of clay in Jewish folklore. It was supposed to protect people during massacres. Not exactly like Frankenstein here.

"First of all, that's made of plastic—" My voice died in my throat as Ashmedai's fingers clenched tight around the action figure. Frankenstein's head popped off with such force, the part catapulted across the room. I ducked to avoid being hit by it.

"You decapitated him," I said in horror.

Casually, Ashmedai dropped the mangled remains of the action figure—a twisted lump of plastic and metal. Gazing me coldly in the eye, he said, "You must be a very powerful tzaddik to be able to create such a being."

I stuttered for a response. "It… It's not…"

"How did you summon me?"

"That was limited edition," I squeaked. "It was a collector's item."

His lips tugged back, revealing the sharp edges of his teeth. In the red glow of the streetlamp, they gleamed as lethally as his hooked black talons. "Answer the question, tzaddik."

"I'm not a tzaddik. I don't even know what that is!"

"Then how did you call me?"

I gulped. "The ring."

His eyes narrowed. "Ring?"

Our gazes landed on the ring at the same time, where it lay on my bed. I made a dash for it, but Ashmedai was one step ahead of me, and as his fingers closed around the ring, my hand cinched around the golden bracelet on his wrist. The metal was searingly hot to the touch, so hot that a wave of white light blanketed my vision. I felt myself suddenly hurled back with such force that even my stomach seemed to flip head-over-heels. When I opened my eyes, I was standing in the center of a vast room lined with stone pillars. Wall sconces contained torches whose flames rippled and danced in the dry breeze that passed between the columns.

A man sat on a gilded throne before me, his keen, dark eyes piercing into mine. He was old enough to be my dad, but unlike my dad, there was a hardness to his features, something unforgiving about the set of his jaw and his chiseled brow bone. He wore a white tunic much like the one that Ashmedai wore, but longer and billowy, its hems decorated with blue embroidery.

He extended his hand to me. Rings dripped from his fingers—glistening bands studded with garnets and sapphires, and upon his index finger, the same ring that the flea market seller had fished from a sea bass's belly.

"Do you know why I have brought you here, demon?"

A low growl erupted from deep within me. Chains rattled, accompanied by the dry rustling of feathers scraping against stone. I fought to look down, but I couldn't even move. My feet were frozen to the ground.

"We will build wonderful things, you and I." He smiled at me. "We will construct a great temple."

Then, just as violently, I was hurled back into my dark bedroom. My stomach churned like I'd taken a corkscrew rollercoaster ride on a belly full of cotton candy and fry bread, and the sour taste of desert sand lingered on my tongue. Across from me, Ashmedai stared back. His palm was warm over mine, but it was a human kind of warmth, and the gold bracelet had gone cold beneath my fingers.

"What did you see?" he whispered, his face stricken.

"A man. He looked like someone important." I thought back to what the robed man had said. He hadn't spoken to me in English, but somehow, I had understood him perfectly. "Was that your memory?"

Ashmedai's only answer was to yank his hand out from under mine. As I picked up the ring, he eyed me warily like he was afraid I might bite. I slipped it into my pocket for safekeeping.

"If you're this ring's guardian, then who does it belong to?" I asked carefully.

His lips curved in a razor-thin smile, revealing a hint of sharp teeth. "You now, apparently."

"Who did it belong to in the past?"

"There have been many owners throughout the centuries," he said levelly, in the same tone my mom used when Naomi started asking too many stupid questions. "And many still to come."

"Okay, but who—"

"Enough questions. I'm tired, human." He settled onto the edge of my bed. "Prepare a chamber for me so that I may rest."

"First of all, my name's Zach," I said. "Second, we don't have a guest bedroom."

"I suppose this will do." Ashmedai sighed, stretching out on the mattress. When he unfurled a wing to its full span, I ducked in time to avoid getting slapped by it. "Zechariah, is it?"

"No, just Zach. It's short for Zachary, but no one calls me that. Do you go by Ash or just Ashmedai?" His name felt strange and unfamiliar on my tongue, like the Hebrew prayers I stumbled over on the rare Friday nights we bothered to light Shabbat candles. I had to try twice before getting it right.

"I go by Your Highness," he said dryly. "But since you can't even manage Ashmedai, then Ash will do."

"Ash then." I wasn't thrilled at sleeping on the floor, but it seemed a little less dangerous than trying to reclaim my bed. "I guess you can spend the night here, but my mom and dad can't find out about you, okay? So, don't make a lot of noise."

The only response was the soft rumble of his belly. We listened to it for an awkward moment before he slowly sat up.

"I'm hungry," he stated.

No way. I had seen enough scary movies to know how this was about to go. I took a step back, eyeing the needle-sharp points of his teeth.

"Just so you know, I taste pretty nasty," I said before he could get any ideas. "Best-case scenario, I'll give you diarrhea."

He shot me a sour look. "Trust me, I've seen piles of donkey dung that look more appetizing than you."

Ouch, that was rough.

"So, you don't eat humans?"

Ash snorted. "Why would I eat humans?"

"Or at least their souls then?"

"Why do you people think your souls are some sort of delicacy?" He scoffed. "If I had a shekel for every time someone asked me that, I'd be richer than King Solomon himself."

I was slightly disappointed. For a demon king, he was doing an awfully poor job of acting like one.

"What do you like to eat then?" I asked.

"I don't eat fish," he said plainly, kicking out his taloned feet. "Or birds."

"I could understand birds, but why not fish?"

He bristled. "That's none of your business, human."

Jeez, he didn't have to be rude about it. It was just a question.

"I'll see what we have in the fridge," I said. "I can't promise you a feast, but I'm sure there are some tasty leftovers."

I headed to the door, then hesitated and looked back. Ash remained seated, his wings sprawled across the blanket like rivers of ink. The streetlights caught on his tined crown and jeweled sash, but left his face carved in shadows, except for the eerie glow of his golden eyes.

5

DOWNSTAIRS, A FAINT blue light shone from the living room. I peeked into the room, where my parents were watching one of their late-night medical dramas. I couldn't remember the title, only that it was something hospital related like *Masks* or *Gauze*. My dad had started snoring in his armchair, and from the way Mom stared slack-jawed at the TV, I was pretty sure she was moments away from falling into a boredom-induced coma. I'd never understand how you could film a show in a hospital, use scalpels for props, and *not* turn it into a horror movie.

"Mom?"

She stirred like I'd roused her from a deep sleep and glanced over at me. "Zach, what are you still doing up?"

"I was just wondering, um, have you heard of Ashmedai before?"

"Ashmedai?" she repeated blankly.

"Yeah, the, uh, king of demons. There's a movie coming out

about him in October, and I guess it's based on a Jewish legend or something. It's PG-13, don't worry."

"Oh. *Oh.*" Recognition brightened her gaze, and she sat up straight. "You're pronouncing the name wrong—"

"Yeah, I get that a lot."

"—but if I recall, there *is* a legend about Ashmedai. You know King Solomon, don't you?"

"Uh, sort of."

"When King Solomon decided to build the First Temple, he didn't want to resort to using blades to cut the stones, because they're basically weapons and the temple was a holy place. He learned that the demon king Ashmedai knew the location of the shamira, an artifact capable of cutting through stone, so he tricked Ashmedai into revealing its location and then helping in the building of the First Temple."

A shiver passed through me. The vision I'd had when I touched Ashmedai's cuff had been real. It had been a memory, not a dream. And that man who'd peered down from the throne with his lips curled in a cold smile—he could have only been King Solomon.

"Why would King Solomon want a demon to help build a temple?" I asked. "Isn't that even worse than using weapons to build one?"

Mom chuckled. "You'd think, but calling Ashmedai a demon or the king of demons is too simplistic. You know how there isn't the same concept of heaven and hell in Judaism as there is in Christianity?"

"Yeah, I guess."

"It's the same with Ashmedai. In Christianity, he's called Asmodeus."

I groaned inwardly. I knew that name from horror movies. "So, you're telling me I've basically—" *Summoned*, I was going to say, but quickly caught myself midsentence. I cleared my throat. "So, you're saying Ashmedai is basically a prince of hell?"

Mom cocked her head, studying me carefully. I gulped. I knew that look. She used it whenever she was trying to figure out if it was me or my dad who left the toilet seat up, or who ate the last cookie, or what had happened to the spare change in the laundry room jar. Sometimes, I was pretty sure that moms were capable of telepathy.

"Yes," she said at last. "In Christian tradition. But our stories aren't as black-and-white. Ashmedai is described as the king of demons, but the word they use in the legends isn't *demons*, it's *shedim*. Compared to demons, shedim are more ambiguous."

"Mom, big-word alert," I said. When Mom got started on a topic related to Jewish folklore or history, she forgot that I was twelve and began talking like a scientist.

Ever since my grandma had died, Mom had been obsessed with the subject. That was what started the whole Judaica hoard. She began looking into who our ancestors were and where they'd come from, and her search had taken her on a wild goose chase—immigration records with misspelled names and birth places, small Jewish towns that had vanished during the war, and sometimes no records at all. All I knew was that her side of the family had come from somewhere in Belarus, which had once been part of the Russian Empire, and before that had been part of Poland, and before *that* had been part of something called Black Ruthenia. In place of those solid facts, she'd filled in her history by focusing on what she could find out—what it meant to be Jewish during that time, what the folklore was, the culture, the history and bloodshed.

Mom chuckled. "By *ambiguous*, I meant that shedim can be good or they can be evil. They're like humans, or like djinni in Islamic folklore. In fact, in the legends, Ashmedai was said to have followed the Torah, and that he'd go up to heaven each day to study and debate with the angels."

Well, that made me feel a little better. If the angels could tolerate Ashmedai, that meant he couldn't be too bad, right? I mean, I was pretty sure angels were allergic to evil and that hellfire made them break out in hives.

Mom yawned, her gaze trailing back to the TV screen. "Anyway, it's getting late, Zach. You should go back to bed."

"Yeah, I'm just going to get a drink first."

"Okay. Good night." She settled into the nook of the couch and turned her attention back to her show.

"Night, Mom."

Once I was sure she had retreated into her TV trance, I went into the kitchen. Cracking open the fridge, I sorted through the shelves and sighed. I doubted even a demon's stomach would be able to handle my mom's hummus wraps or bran muffins, while the takeout from last week looked like it was in the process of breeding strange, new organisms. In the bottom drawer, I unearthed the fuzzy remains of what had likely once been an orange—like, five weeks ago.

Groaning, I wiped my hand on my shirt. That left the half-eaten rotisserie chicken or last night's cheese pizza. Ash probably considered birds to be his close cousins, so Domino's it was. Since my parents would hear if I used the microwave, I plated the two slices cold and brought them back to my room.

Ash was studying the surviving action figures lined up on the shelf, most likely deciding which one he wanted to destroy next. He glanced my way as I entered. "If these aren't golems, are they idols?"

"As in *American Idol*?"

He stared at me as if I were an idiot, which I had a feeling wasn't too far from the truth. "Do people worship these?"

"Uh, no. Not unless they really love horror movies. They're called action figures." I took the figurine from his hand. "This one is Dracula. He's a vampire, so he drinks people's blood. Creepy, right?"

"No, not really. He just looks like a weak human." Ash eyed Dracula's black cloak. "One with horrible taste in fashion."

"That's because you haven't seen the movies," I said, then remembered that I was talking to not just your run-of-the-mill demon, but the literal king of demons. He probably would find Dracula to be as scary as a bologna sandwich, and that was being generous.

"Anyway, I brought you pizza," I said, handing him the plate.

Ash picked up a slice and flopped it hesitantly in his hand.

"It's good, trust me."

He took a small bite, chewed, and swallowed. Once he realized that it was actually edible, he practically engulfed a slice, pausing only to lick the grease from his fingertips. "This pizza, you call it, where can I get more? It must be very expensive to be this good. A true delicacy."

"Actually, not really. It's nothing special. You can buy it at a grocery store, or even a gas station."

The second slice of pizza disappeared within moments. I was a little nervous that he'd ask for more and I'd have to break the news to him that he'd eaten the last two slices. Maybe then human souls would start looking tasty after all.

Instead, as soon as the final bit of crust vanished into his stomach—if demons did, in fact, have stomachs and not just bottomless pits—Ash shoved the plate over to the other side of the bed and collapsed on his back with a groan, clearly in a food coma. His toes curled in satisfaction, talons snagging on the blanket.

"That has to be the most delicious thing I've eaten in the last three hundred years," he said, placing a hand over his stomach.

"Where were you before this?" I asked as he stretched out.

The only response was a shameless belch.

I groaned. There was the smell of sulfur and brimstone. I took a few steps away to get out of range, then retrieved my sleeping bag from my closet's bottom shelf. Naomi had taken it to Girl Scout camp last summer and had returned it stinking of grilled cheese and pond water, with a suspicious hint of bedwetting. Ugh, it still smelled the same. This was the last time I was going to have a sleepover with a demon.

"New York," he said as I rolled out the sleeping bag. When I glanced back, his gaze had drifted to the ceiling, and a distant look came over his features. "I awoke on a steamship. That was the last time someone called me. Everything before that and everything after—those moments in between—it's just like dreaming. Sometimes, I hear things, or see things, or feel what the wearer is feeling and know what they know, but other times, there's nothing but sinking."

"Does the ring control you then?" I asked.

He scoffed. "Do you think that I, the king of demons, would be so weak that a stupid trinket could hold any power over me? Don't make me laugh, human. I simply have a vested interest in the ring. It belonged to King Solomon, and now that he is dead, it belongs to me. But I suppose I'll let you hold on to it for a while. If humans have such short lives, what are a few more years?"

I didn't really like his tone of voice. "I plan to live to at least a hundred, thank you."

He rolled his eyes. "A hundred is nothing in the span of a demon's lifetime."

His words rang false. More likely, he couldn't take the ring by force. He just had to wait for me to give it to him.

"You know, if it's that old, it's probably worth something," I said, sitting on my sleeping bag. "Maybe I should just sell it."

He hoisted himself up and stared at me in disbelief. "Are you that foolish? It's worth far more than just money. Besides, the last thing I want to do is end up in the service of some..." He trailed off.

"You have to stay with the ring, don't you?" I asked.

Ash bristled, but his silence was answer enough.

"It doesn't control me," he said at last. "But yes, we share a connection. Where it goes, I go. I don't want to stray far from it. Perhaps it's simple nostalgia."

"What were you doing up until now? Were you trapped in the ring?"

His brow furrowed in annoyance.

"No, I was just..." He hesitated, and for the first time, I caught a trace of unease in his features. "I was just sleeping."

"Sleeping," I repeated.

"You humans get so boring, it's the only way I can pass the time. After a while, you get tired of all the drama. Battles, and inquisitions, and rulers. Once you've seen one king, you've seen them all."

"I guess so." I didn't agree, but what did I know? "So, the ring woke you up then?"

"Yes. Now, enough idle chatter." He lay down again with a huff. "Let me sleep."

I decided not to push him. I could tell that he was already upset, and the last thing I wanted to do was piss off a demon, ambiguous intentions or not.

As he rolled over onto his back, I sat on the sleeping bag for a minute or two longer, a little afraid to turn my back on him. In all the movies, after the villain was defeated, they returned for a last-minute scare. Sure, the only devious things Ash had done so far was steal my bed and decapitate one of my prized collectibles, but I was still half-convinced that souls were demons' version of caviar.

"Ash, you awake?"

When Ash didn't answer, I repeated his name a second time. He shifted onto his stomach, mumbling in a foreign language. One wing unfurled and came within inches of knocking me flat on my back.

I waited for a moment longer before lying down on the sleeping bag. If I zipped myself up, he might mistake me for a human burrito in his sleep, so I tugged the flap over myself but left it open at the seam.

"Good night, Ash." I rolled over onto my side and drew the sleeping bag blanket up to my neck.

Silence. As I drifted off, my fingers strayed to the ring in my pocket. Even now, the gold band radiated a soft, unnatural warmth, lulling me into a deep sleep.

6

THAT NIGHT, I dreamed of talking dogs and bird kings. When I woke, I blinked in the streams of sunlight pouring through the window, and for a perfect moment, I thought it was all a dream. Then I rolled over and groaned at the ache in my back. Sleeping on the floor was brutal. Next time I visited Grandma and Grandpa, I'd have to ask Clarence how he tolerated it. Then again, knowing my grandparents, he probably had a goose-down dog bed designed by Gucci or something.

I lifted my head. "Ash, you awake?"

No response. From where I lay, I couldn't see much more than my striped comforter and the edge of the pillow.

Maybe it had been a dream after all. Although that didn't explain why I'd decided to haul out the camping gear.

I rose to my feet. The blankets had been kicked aside and bulged in a pile at the foot of the bed. In the center of the mound lay a single black feather.

Swallowing back the boulder that lodged in my throat, I hurried from the room. Voices filtered through the walls. Holding my breath, I peeked through the kitchen doorway.

My parents were already at the kitchen table. Dad had started a new fad diet where he didn't eat breakfast until noon, so he miserably sipped his cup of black coffee, eyeing Mom's waffles and sliced fruit like a mogwai on the verge of turning into a gremlin.

"Hey, Zach," Dad said as I stepped into the room. "Was that you or Naomi banging around up there?"

My mouth went dry. "Um, what?"

"Just a few minutes ago."

Then I heard it—the faint tread of feet on carpet, and a raspy whisper like feathers scraping against plaster. Uh-oh.

"Toilet!" I said quickly and darted from the room. As I entered the hall, my breath caught in my throat. Ash was nowhere in sight. So, what had I heard just now?

Farther down the hall, a clawed footprint appeared in the carpet. Then another.

"Ash," I hissed, glowering into the thin air. "Get back to my room."

The footprints drew closer and closer. Palms moist, I took a step back, a twinge of fear building in my chest. What if it wasn't Ash after all? What if the ring had summoned more than just one demon?

Closer.

The presence slipped past me, close enough that coarse feathers brushed against my forearm, and then he was gone. I

50

turned to watch the footprints continue down the hall, before disappearing as they reached the kitchen doorway.

Not good. So not good. Pivoting on my heel, I rushed back into the kitchen and skidded to a stop in front of the table.

"What's wrong, Zach?" Mom asked, furrowing her brow. She lowered the chunk of pineapple she had speared. "Your face is all red. Are you sick?"

"No. I..." I scanned the room, searching for any sign of him. My panic must have been enough to convince Ash to move on tiptoes, because the only sound I heard was my own pounding heartbeat. "I just have a stomachache."

"That's what you get for eating cold hot dogs," Dad said with a chuckle, earning a withering look from my mom.

"Can I get you anything?" she asked. "Maybe something light, like toast? With the field trip tomorrow, hopefully you're not coming down with something."

Movement in the corner of my eye drew my gaze across the room. Hidden from my parents' view by the kitchen's divider wall, the door to the fridge creaked open. I held my breath, watching in mute horror as a jar of pickles levitated in the air, the lid unscrewing on its own.

"Zach?" My mom raised her eyebrows.

"I'm just going to see what's in the fridge. You two relax, enjoy your breakfast." I tried to smile, but I was pretty sure it came out lopsided. "I'm twelve, Mom. I know how to make toast."

I hurried past, reaching the fridge just as the pickle jar slid back onto the shelf, sloshing juice across the plastic tray. Ziploc bags of baby carrots rustled. A single bran muffin rose in the air and got a bite chomped out of it by invisible teeth.

Sweat dripped down the back of my neck. Hesitantly, I reached out, testing the air until my fingertips brushed against silk. I grasped onto the fabric, felt Ash tense, heard the soft whish of feathers.

"What are you doing?" I whispered frantically. "Mom and Dad are out there. They can't see this."

"I'm hungry." Ash's voice came out muffled through a mouthful of bran muffin. "What is this strange bread?"

Moist crumbs flew in my face. I grimaced and swatted them away. For someone older than the earth's creation, he ate like a toddler.

"You need to go back to my room." I cast a nervous glance behind me, certain that at any moment, my mom or dad would rise from the table and step around the partition. "I'll get you whatever you want to eat, just please, go back. You'll give my parents heart attacks, and I'm too young to be an orphan."

Before he could respond, the rapid patter of footsteps came from the hall. I snagged the floating muffin just as Naomi barreled into the kitchen.

"Waffles!" she whooped, before turning to me and scrunching up her nose at the muffin I held in one outstretched arm. "Ew, Zach. Why are you eating *that*?"

Slowly, I lowered my arm. "Uh, I could use the bran?"

"For what?" Then she groaned. "Oh, wait. No. I don't want to know."

"Because I—"

"No." Scrunching up her face, she pressed her hands over her ears. "I'm not listening!"

"—have to poop," I finished, earning another dramatic groan from her.

As she sat down at the table, I put the muffin on the counter and closed the fridge. There was nothing in there Ash would want to eat anyway, but maybe there was something in the pantry I could get him.

Going over, I searched the pantry's shelves. I stowed two oatmeal cookies in the pocket of my pajama pants and slipped an unopened box of Ritz crackers beneath my shirt. When I turned to the kitchen, I was relieved to find the fridge as I had left it, although all that remained of the muffin was its crumpled paper liner.

On the way out, I snagged my phone from the charger by the sink. Naomi unintentionally kept my parents distracted by telling them about a dream she had last night involving a purple elephant and a floating castle lifted by balloons. I slipped out the door before they could notice my stolen food.

Ash was sitting on my bed when I entered my room, his hands and feet still slightly see-through. As I watched, color returned to his limbs. I hadn't noticed before, but his nails were a dark smoky brown, curved into hooked points.

"Never do that again," I said, hurling one of the oatmeal cookies at him. He caught it with ease and tore open the wrapper.

"Sorry." He crammed the entire cookie into his mouth and continued to talk, spewing crumbs everything. "I waited for you to wake up, but you humans sleep for so long. Mmm. This is delicious. What is it?"

"An oatmeal cookie. I brought you Ritz crackers too." After placing the box on the bed, I checked my phone. Sandra had texted me an hour ago, asking when she should come over. On second thought, maybe it would be better if we met somewhere where there weren't nosy little sisters.

I texted Sandra, telling her that I would meet her at the park in an hour, before helping myself to the other cookie.

"Listen, we're going to meet my friend, but I can't have you go around invisible or with your wings hanging out. Can't you try looking like a regular boy?"

He rolled his eyes. "What do you think? Even the weakest of shedim are capable of hiding their true nature. Believe it or not, but for several years, I assumed King Solomon's form and ruled Jerusalem in his place. His subjects had no idea, not the faintest clue who I was. It was fun at first, but resolving the arguments of rival shepherds gets old after a while. Even for me."

"Where was King Solomon during this?"

He laughed. "Oh, I threw him four hundred leagues across the continent. When he came back, he was furious. You should've seen it. It was hilarious."

I gulped. Yeah, that didn't sound very funny to me.

"Behold, human." He lifted a hand. "The power of a sheyd."

The black feathers disintegrated into shadow, as if they were nothing more than smoke to begin with. The unnatural gold gleam of his eyes faded, leaving them a soft shade of honey.

When he grinned, his teeth were no longer sharp, but like any human's. Even his fingernails had dulled and lightened.

"Is this better?" he asked.

"Almost. You'll need new clothes."

"Is that so?" He smirked, brushing his hands down his front. The silk coarsened beneath his fingers, his garment's draped folds receding into a black T-shirt and then black jeans below that. The gold embroidery remained on his shirtsleeves and pant legs, but was two-dimensional now, like it had been screen printed on. As for his jeweled belt and crown, they simply wisped away in the same manner as his wings.

I stared slack-jawed at him. "H-how?"

"Have you forgotten what I am, human?"

Unable to help myself, I reached out and touched his sleeve. It looked like cotton, but underneath my fingers, the fabric was much softer and sheer. Silk, or something even finer.

Stepping back, I eyed his bird-clawed feet. His talons flexed and sunk into the carpet. "Can you hide those, too?"

"No. We shedim are known by our claws."

"Let me try to find something." Sighing, I rummaged through the closet until I uncovered a pair of sneakers my grandma had bought me when she'd visited a few months ago. They were a size too big for me, but his taloned feet fit them perfectly.

As he tied the laces, I glanced down at his gold bracelet. "If you're not going to hide that like your crown, why don't you take it off and keep it here? It looks expensive."

Ash flinched, his hand straying over the ornament, as if he had just become aware of it.

"No," he said, warily.

"Don't worry. Nobody goes into my room. It'll be safe here."

"I can't. Take it off, that is. Or transmute it."

I blinked. "Why?"

"It's...stuck."

"Stuck?" I peered at it. It was hinged, and in the front, there was a little hole, like there was once a push button there. Maybe after a few thousand years, the mechanism had rusted shut. Before I could take a closer look, Ash rose to his feet and crossed his arms.

"Now, shall we?" he said dryly.

Oh well, people would just think he liked shiny things. I looked him over. With his wings and talons hidden, he looked a little more convincing. At least enough to get us to the park.

OUTSIDE, THE SUN beamed down, and a pleasant breeze rustled the fronds of the palm tree that screened our yard. I walked for several blocks, listening to the muffled tread of footsteps behind me.

"I think we're good now," I said, once we made it some distance from home.

Ash materialized on the sidewalk. Leaves swirled around his feet as he appeared, and my skin tingled like the air was filled with static electricity.

"Where are we going?" he asked.

"The park."

"Park," he repeated thoughtfully.

"A park is a—"

"I can assure you, I know what a park is," Ash said bombastically. "How dare you question my intelligence, human."

I stammered for a response. "N-no, not at all. I just thought…"

"I attended Queen Victoria's Golden Jubilee in Hyde Park," he proclaimed. "I was there when King Louis XIV raised the Gardens of Versailles. I helped *build* the Hanging Gardens of Babylon. I am—"

"Immortal. Yeah, I know."

He huffed as we continued on our way. "Yes."

I couldn't enjoy the bright summer day with Ash practically breathing down the back of my neck. For a demon, he had no concept of personal bubbles. When I stopped walking, he nearly slammed into my back.

I swiveled around. "Ash, you're in my space."

"And what space is that?" he asked earnestly, looking around as if he expected there to be a sign.

"Just don't walk so close."

He fell back a few steps. "Is this better?"

"Better," I conceded.

"You'll have to forgive me if I forget my manners. It's been a while since I've been around humans. Especially the short ones."

I bristled. "I'm perfectly average for my age."

"All humans are short compared to me," he boasted, earning a snort and a roll of my eyes.

"I hate to break it to you, Ash, but you're not exactly Godzilla." I measured him with my gaze. "We're practically the same height."

He smirked. "Bold of you to assume that, Zechariah."

"It's Zach," I reminded, before frowning as his words dawned on me. "Wait, what's that supposed to mean?"

"This form is simply one that is…" A strange look passed over his face, and his smirk slowly faded. Furrowing his brow, he turned away. "Soothing."

"What is it?" I asked. "What's wrong?"

"It's nothing." He chuckled, but the sound was flatter now. Restlessly, he traced his fingertips over his garnet-studded bracelet, a hint of worry shadowing his gaze. "I was just remembering something an old friend once told me."

As we neared the park, I rehearsed in my head how exactly I was going to break the news to Sandra. I couldn't imagine how she'd react if I tried telling her I'd made friends with a demon, except that it would probably involve an exorcist.

At this hour, the park bustled with life. Little kids covered every surface imaginable, zinging like Ping-Pong balls across the playground. I kept to the outskirts to avoid being trampled. By the way Ash grimaced at the squeals and laughter, I suspected he feared death by toddler too.

Sandra sat by the duck pond, tossing chunks of a granola bar into the water. A few strands of black hair had come free of her sharp bob, framing her dark brown eyes and bold, downcast brows. If her scowl wasn't enough to scare the little kids away, her grungy hoodie and ripped jeans were adorned with enough safety pins that the threat of tetanus made parents keep a wide berth.

"Wait here," I told Ash, pausing at the nearby gazebo. "If I tell her about you and the ring at the same time, her head will explode."

"Don't take long. I don't enjoy waiting."

As I approached, Sandra cast the last piece of granola bar to the ducks and scrunched up the wrapper. She made sure to toss it in the recycling bin, not the trash can like everyone else. When I walked home with her after school, she would always take a plastic bag with her to pick up the litter. With how often she talked about saving the planet, I was pretty sure that she was destined to become the kind of activist who chained themselves to endangered trees and torpedoed oil rigs. Come to think of it, this ring would probably become a nightmare in her hands too.

"Took you long enough." She rolled her eyes. "Don't tell me you stopped to throw more hotdogs at pigeons along the way. You know they aren't supposed to eat human food, right?"

I took a deep breath. "Look, I didn't cause the gullnado yesterday by throwing a hotdog at one. This is going to sound crazy, but I found a magic ring that lets me talk to animals, and I might have lied to the birds about giving them food. There were so many of them. I didn't think they'd all want chips."

Sandra listened to me gravely. She was able to keep a straight face until I reached the end, which was when she burst into laughter until tears popped in her eyes. "Oh, Zach, you can't possibly expect me to believe that you have a magic ring."

I winced. "Yeah, that's kind of what I was hoping you would believe."

"Is this like that time you pretended your sister's American Girl doll had come to life like the dummy from *Goosebumps*?"

My cheeks heated up. I wished she'd quit reminding me of that. "That was in fourth grade, Sandra, and in my defense, I'd say there was a good fifty percent chance that doll was demonically possessed. I know it sounds ridiculous, but it's true this time. Just let me show you."

"I can show her," Ash volunteered hopefully, strolling over from the gazebo. I shook my head. The last thing I needed was for him to transform in broad daylight and create another viral video. I could just imagine the hashtags.

"Who's this?" Sandra asked, her gaze lingering on him. Normally, her death stares were enough to put even Jeffrey and his crew on edge, but Ash just returned it, playing chicken until she looked away, her cheeks reddening.

"I'll tell you in a minute. But first, I want to show you the ring." As I took it from my pocket, I could feel Ash's gaze burning into me. If he stared at me any harder, I was a little afraid his eyes would shoot lasers.

"You should be careful with that thing," Ash said warily as I placed the ring in her hand. "It's not a toy."

"Yeah, I kind of figured that out when I nearly started seagull Armageddon." I rolled my eyes. "Don't worry, we'll be careful."

Sandra slipped the ring onto her finger. It was too big for her too, and she had to grip it tightly in her fist.

"What now?" she asked.

"Talk to a bird or something," I said. "Just don't tell them you have any food, or it won't be pretty."

Still smirking, she looked around until she found a suitable target—a pigeon feasting on the remains of a hamburger.

"Hey, bird," she said.

61

I couldn't tell how the pigeon answered, but her mouth fell open and she stared at it in amazement.

"No way," she whispered. "That bird just called me a bad name."

"Yeah, birds are rude." Maybe that was where the phrase "flip someone the bird" came from.

"Fine," Sandra said to the pigeon. "Go enjoy your hamburger. I hope it gives you diarrhea."

The pigeon flew off with an indignant squawk, and I ducked just in case it decided to get revenge on us. Sandra turned to me, her eyes gleaming with excitement.

"Okay, it's a magic ring," she said, handing the ring back to me.

"Told you so."

"Where'd you get it?"

"At the flea market. Some old man sold it to me for twenty dollars."

She turned to Ash. "And this is…?"

"Ashmedai, the king of demons. But I just call him Ash."

She nodded slowly, her eyes glazing over.

"He's the guardian of the ring," I added helpfully. "I, uh, might have accidentally summoned him."

"Zach, can I have a word with you in private?" she asked with a strained smile.

"Sure," I said, and she dragged me over to the shade of the gazebo.

She glanced back nervously in Ash's direction. "The king of demons, Zach? Really? So, you're making friends with demons now?"

"Well, I didn't really have a choice. He came with the ring. It's a two-for-one deal."

"I hate to break it to you, Zach, but I don't think a deal with a demon has ever ended well. I'm pretty sure that's how people get cursed."

"Come on, Sandra, isn't eternal damnation worth it?" I said, but she didn't even crack a smile. Despite the rumors that flew around school about her being a witch, her family was seriously Catholic. Instead of collecting whatever kitschy Judaica she could get her hands on, *Sandra's* mom kept a home altar, complete with a crucifix, candles in tiny red glasses, and a framed painting of Saint Mariana holding a lily and a skull. Her family actually went to church, and not just for the big holidays. For the first time, I realized that Sandra might actually believe in all that fire and brimstone, that it wasn't just a scene out of Hollywood for her.

It made me feel a bit heavy in the throat. Sandra was the only one I'd come out to. She'd told me more than once she didn't believe being gay was a sin, but I was a little afraid what she thought deep down.

"We should take the ring to a priest or something," Sandra said as I slipped the ring back into my pocket.

"No priests," I said, a bit sharper than I intended.

"A rabbi then."

I groaned. "No rabbis either. That's just as bad."

"But, Zach, there's no way we can deal with this ourselves."

"Look, let's just have fun with it for a few days. What's the worst that could happen?"

She rolled her eyes. "Oh yes, what's the worst that could happen with a ring that belongs to the king of hell?"

"King of demons," I corrected her.

"Is there a difference?"

"I'm not sure," I admitted. "My mom said that shedim like Ash can be good or evil, just like people."

"Either way, it's perfectly harmless, I'm sure," she said sarcastically.

"I can use this ring to impress Dominic," I said, "or get back at Jeffrey. Sandra, this ring could change my life."

"Or end it," she said gravely, glancing over at where Ash waited. "For all you know, using the ring could drag you down to hell too."

I snorted.

"I'm serious."

"I hate to break it to you, but people my whole life have told me I'm going to hell," I said before I could stop myself. The anger in my voice took me off guard. I exhaled slowly, trying again in a quieter tone. "It's not just... It's not just liking boys, Sandra. Do you know the first time I got told I was going to end up in hell? It was in second grade, when my mom and I were shopping in the Hanukkah section of the grocery store. We were just buying some stupid menorah candles, and this woman came up to us and said that if we didn't accept Jesus, we were going to burn in a lake of fire for all eternity. I was eight, and she looked me in the face, and she said it. I was eight."

The frustration drained from her gaze. "Zach..."

64

I took a deep breath. "So, yeah, maybe Ash is evil, but what does that make me?"

"You're not evil, Zach."

"I just…" My voice warbled, and I had to swallow hard, angry at the lump building in my throat. "If there's an underworld, I might as well score brownie points with the king of demons while I still can, you know?"

She laughed helplessly. "Zach, with your sense of humor, you'll get kicked out of there within twenty-four hours."

Hearing her laugh made me feel a little better about saying what I really meant. "I want to worry about what I can change, Sandra. And I know this: if using the ring can change my life for the better, it doesn't matter where it came from."

Sandra hesitated. She knew what it was like to be bullied. It was one of the reasons we had become friends. For her, it was because she was Latinx, so naturally, the mouth breathers like Jeffrey assumed she was Mexican, even though for world heritage day, she had brought in slices of milhoja, layered with puff pastry and caramel sauce and decorated with mini yellow-blue-and-red Ecuadorian flags.

Jeffrey had used every opportunity he had to bully her, even more viciously than he did with me, spouting crap about walls and borders, and making fun of her mom's accent or her packed lunches. Whenever it was his turn to do roll call, he'd call her Sandra Tamale instead of Tomala, never mind that Ecuadorian tamales were called humitas.

The worst part was that, like with me, the teachers did nothing about it. Our homeroom teacher had stopped correcting

Jeffrey the third time he said Tamale, and just smiled like she thought it was a joke we were all in on. I didn't get it. I knew that the teachers knew. They had to. You couldn't be a teacher and be that unobservant, right? I mean, even jellyfish had more common sense than that, and they didn't even have eyes!

"Come on, Sandra," I said. "If we don't stop Jeffrey, nobody will."

Sandra gave me a long, lingering look before sighing in defeat. "Oh, all right."

I perked up. "So, you'll help me think of a way to use the ring?"

"Yeah, what are friends for?" She nudged me lightly with her elbow. "But I will say this, Zach Darlington—if teaming up with a demon king lands us both in hell, you'd better watch out, because it won't be demons down there whooping your butt. It'll be me."

I grinned as she feigned a one-two punch. "I'm scared already."

"As you should be."

8

AS WE RETURNED to the gazebo, my stomach plummeted. Ash was gone.

"He was here just a minute ago," I said, my voice cracking. "Where'd he go?"

"Don't panic," Sandra said. "He has to be around here somewhere."

We tore through the park, shouting his name. He wasn't by the jungle gym or even by the skating area. Babysitting Naomi was bad enough. If I'd known that I had to babysit a demon too, I never would've bought the ring in the first place.

On my way back to the duck pond, I crossed over the grass to shorten the trip. I was so busy looking for Ash, I didn't pay attention to where I was going, and collided with a woman standing under one of the bay trees. With her black slacks and matching polo, she blended into the shadows. She'd been standing so still, I might've mistaken her for a mannequin if she hadn't grunted as I knocked shoulders with her.

I skidded to a halt in front of her, mortified. "I'm so sorry."

"Careful now." A strange, flat smile crept across her lips. "You should watch where you're going."

"I know. I was just searching for a friend. Sorry again."

"Kids get hurt when they're not paying attention." Her eyes were wide and glassy, staring at me unblinkingly. "They get run over by cars. They fall into open manholes."

"Uh, thanks for the warning, I guess." Not that I'd want to go down one of those manholes anyway. The one near our house smelled like a Porta Potty, and if the stench was any indicator, I'd bet anything San Pancras's sewer tunnels were crawling with alligators and vampires.

When the woman didn't respond, I continued on my way. Sandra waited awkwardly on the sidewalk. As I joined her, I glanced back at the woman.

She remained where she stood, that creepy smile fixed to her lips like a ventriloquist dummy's. There was a patch sewed onto her polo, so maybe she was a park worker. Still, with the way she was staring at us, I figured it'd only be a matter of time before she exchanged her uniform for a *Scream* mask and a butcher's knife.

"Any luck?" I asked Sandra as we continued down the sidewalk.

She shook her head. "Do you think he ran off?"

Just as I thought about trying to use the ring to call him, Ash broke away from the swarm of kids surrounding an ice-cream truck idling by the parking lot and strode over to us.

"Isn't this amazing?" he said, showing us the ice-cream cone that he had somehow acquired. "It's cold like ice and yet it's perfectly round. Just a century, the only ice you humans had, you scraped from the surfaces of frozen lakes. But it's the dead of summer. How did you manage such a feat?"

Sandra groaned.

"How did you get that?" I asked. "You don't even have money."

"I can be very convincing when I need to be."

I looked over at the ice-cream man. He gazed into the distance, his face dead white. The Popsicle he was holding had begun to melt over his hand. It looked like he had seen some things.

I took a deep breath. "Okay, whatever power you just used on him, please don't do that again."

Ash huffed, rolling his eyes. "You know something, Zach? You remind me a bit of Solomon. All work and no play."

"Because I don't want you to obliterate anybody else's brain cells?"

"Yes." Ash took another bite of the ice-cream cone, breaking through the layer of nut-encrusted chocolate. As he ate, he nearly groaned in satisfaction. "Magnificent. In so little time, you humans have invented so much. I'm actually quite impressed, considering God's first few attempts."

"First few attempts?" Sandra asked.

"Well, before he settled on a design, God went through his monkey phase, and before that, his reptile phase. I actually kind of liked that one. I tried to convince him, but eventually Uriel won him over. Just think. If I had gotten my way, you would have tails and scales. Instead—" he glanced me up and down with a rather criticizing look "—you have this."

I scoffed.

"You look like a person too." I glanced around before lowering my voice. "Except for the wings of course."

"Yet again, bold of you to assume that."

I gawked at him. "Wait. Don't tell me you have a tail too."

"No, I am something far more majestic than your common lizard. What you see now is simply a form that is soothing. I'm afraid that you would be unable to comprehend my true form. Others have tried, and it all ended rather badly."

"Can you just give us a hint?" Sandra asked.

His smile faded, and vague disorientation crept across his features. He looked down at his hands, curling his fingers.

"I don't..." He trailed off. "I was asleep for so long, it's all a bit fuzzy. In many ways, the past feels like a long dream. Something that I am just beginning to wake from."

"I'm sorry," I said, which seemed like both the appropriate thing to say and yet totally inadequate.

He shook his head. "It will all come back to me. See, when you have lived as long as I have, what are a few thousand years? Everything loses its distinctions. You meet someone, and they remind you of someone else, and in your memory, they both blur together into the same person. It's very hard to distinguish them when the separate memories begin to merge, even for a sheyd as powerful as me. Do you understand?"

"I think I do," I said, after giving it some thought. Maybe it was a little like deja vu, except his deja vu was actually grounded in reality, in memories that had happened centuries ago.

"So, back to how we're going to use the ring," Sandra said. "How exactly do you plan on impressing Dominic?"

I gave it some thought. "What if we save him from a swarm of pigeons?"

"Do you seriously want to sic a swarm of pigeons on the guy you like?"

"Sandra." I blushed, glancing in Ash's direction. Having already inhaled half the ice-cream cone, he was working his way through the surviving scoop.

He paused midbite as he noticed me staring and lowered the ice-cream cone. "What? Do you want me to get you one too?"

"Thank you, but no." I glanced in the direction of the ice-cream trunk. "I don't think the ice-cream man will be able to survive another encounter."

The man continued to stare open-mouthed into space. As we watched, the melting Popsicle he was holding slipped from its stick and splashed across the blacktop.

"Reconsidering that exorcism, Zach?" Sandra muttered as Ash turned his attention back to his cone.

"We just have to teach Ash how you're supposed to act in society. We need to show him what it means to be human."

"How are we supposed to do that?"

I grinned. "I can think of one way."

9

THE SAN PANCRAS Cinema was one of the town's most famous landmarks, with its geometrical façade and old-fashioned movie signs. Each week it featured one vintage movie in room 2 and a classic horror movie in room 4, the auditorium that was rumored to be haunted. Uncle Jimmy had given me a gift card to the cinema for my twelfth birthday, and there was still enough money left on the card that I was able to buy tickets for all three of us.

With tickets in hand, we made our way into the theater. The air-conditioning felt so great after the bus ride over that I couldn't help but sigh. The marquee sign over the door advertised the 1931 *Frankenstein*, but we'd bought tickets for the PG-rated new release, which we were *totally* going to see.

"Hold your horses, buddy," the ticket checker said as Ash pushed on ahead.

"Do not try me, human," he growled. "I have faced beings

far more powerful than you, stood down kings and angels. I am not a force to be trifled with."

"Er...?" The man blinked, befuddled. His hair bristled from beneath his uniform visor in a blond frizz.

"Ash, he's just doing his job," I said, a bit nervous that a demonic temper tantrum might get us banned from the movie theater. "You have to give him a ticket."

Ash scoffed, handed over the ticket without ripping the man's arm off. I sighed in relief and gave mine over.

"Have you ever had popcorn, Ash?" Sandra asked as we walked over to the concession stand.

"Popcorn," he echoed quietly, and I could tell from his face that he had no idea at all what she meant.

"It's better if we show you," I said.

I didn't want to risk him giving another person brain damage, so Sandra and I pooled together our change. We bought a giant bag of popcorn, and sodas too, and a box of M&M's that we could split between us.

He sampled the candies a bit warily, but after the first taste, quickly crammed more into his mouth.

"Don't eat them all," Sandra said, appalled. "Save some for us."

"You humans never cease to amaze me. Such innovation. You create these amazing things, like this for instance—" He held up one of the M&M's. "A tiny morsel of chocolate enclosed within a hard, colorful shell. Marvelous."

"It's just an M&M," I said. "They make them by the thousands."

"Where?" Ash looked back at the concession stand. "Here?"

"Uh, no. In a factory."

Ash didn't answer, but from the gleam in his eyes, I could tell he was planning the heist of the century. He'd probably eat his way through the candy company's entire stock if he could.

I couldn't really blame him. If the last time he'd awoken was in New York on a steamship, it made sense that things like M&M's would surprise him. My dad told me Victorian times were pretty rough, like apparently some people even pooped themselves to death back then.

Instead of going into the auditorium for the PG comedy, we made our way to room 4. We had arrived ten minutes before *Frankenstein* started and the previews were still showing. The theater was only halfway packed, so we had our choice of seats. After it ended, I figured we could just sneak into the movie being played in the next auditorium over and repeat the process until my mom called me home or we were kicked out.

We found three empty seats in the last row. Sandra liked being right by the aisle, while I picked the one farthest inward.

"So how are we going to get back at Jeffrey?" Sandra asked as we watched an advertisement for Coca-Cola.

As a couple moved into the row in front of us, I lowered my voice. "We'll talk about this later. Let's just watch the movie and let me think."

"I don't see why you can't do both at the same time," Sandra said, and Ash nodded eagerly in agreement.

I sighed. "I'm horrible at multitasking."

The man in the row in front of us turned and cocked his

head. "Aren't you kids a bit too young to be watching this movie?"

Ash opéned his mouth to respond, but I grabbed his shoulder and shook my head. Offering the man a forced smile, I said, "Our parents gave us permission."

"If you say so." The man frowned but looked back at the screen as a new commercial came on.

"Ash, you'll like this movie," I whispered. "It's set in the past, and it's about a scientist who brings a monster to life using body parts from corpses. You know that action figure you destroyed? That's the same monster as in the film. Now you'll be able to see how even monsters try to blend in and don't, uh, eat people or steal their souls."

"I know how people act," Ash said dryly, turning his attention back to the screen. "I've had to deal with you humans for thousands of years. But I suppose…this moving picture is interesting in its own right."

As *Frankenstein* began, I settled back in my seat. This was one of my favorite horror movies, because it wasn't too nasty or too bloody. I hated to admit it, but even the sight of raw chicken grossed me out. Although I loved the heart-racing feeling of a good jump-scare, I didn't like feeling as if I was about to puke.

Even though I'd seen the movie before, I got antsy just from the opening scenes. Fully immersed, I reached into the popcorn bucket and touched its greasy paper bottom.

Flabbergasted, I turned to Ash. "Did you really just eat all the popcorn?"

He paused midway through slurping down *my* Coke. "Yes. It was delicious."

With a groan, I looked over to Sandra. "Where does it all go?"

"I think he has a bottomless pit for a stomach," she whispered back.

The couple in front of us rose and made their way to another row of empty seats, though not before shooting us death glares. I sighed, sinking back against my seat. Ash would empty our entire fridge if I let him.

On the screen, the platform holding the lifeless monster was slowly raised by machinery. Higher, higher, until it reached a hole in the laboratory's roof. Lightning flashed, and thunder trembled the room. When the creature was lowered once more, its arm twitched. A tremor racked its fingers. Delirious with triumph, Dr. Frankenstein screamed, "It's alive!"

"Ash, isn't this so cool?" I asked, turning.

He gripped the armrest so tightly that the plastic cracked beneath his fingers, eyes fixated on the screen. His lips peeled back, revealing a hint of sharp teeth.

"Ash?" I reached for him, but something held me back.

"Don't you think it is profane," he said quietly, almost to himself, "to create a creature for the purpose of doing your bidding? For the sole purpose?"

"That's kind of the point of the movie..."

"Who is meant to be the evil one here?"

I exchanged a look with Sandra.

"Um, it's complicated," she said. "But the monster."

"For being created?"

I swallowed hard. "Ash, are you okay?"

Finally, he looked at me, and he chuckled like it was a joke we'd all been in on. "Why wouldn't I be? I was simply musing how you humans are truly deplorable. You insist on bending everything to your will, and whatever does not kneel, you destroy."

I had no answer to that.

Maybe it was just the jittery black-and-white movie, or the memory of rage and anguish on Ash's face, or the darkness of the theater, but something didn't feel right. As *Frankenstein* continued, I shifted in my seat, my skin prickling with unease.

At the other end of the row, an old woman sat hunched over. The screen's blue light gleamed across her white hair and round glasses. I couldn't see her eyes, or tell if she even *had* eyes, but I couldn't shake the feeling she was watching us.

I flinched as fingers closed around my shoulder and I nearly jumped out of my skin. It was only Ash.

"I have an idea." Lowering his voice, he leaned close enough that his cool breath brushed against the side of my neck. He didn't smell like fire or sulfur. He didn't smell like anything, except maybe the breeze off the ocean, like he'd carried the scent in with him. "I can beat up Jeffrey for you. What do you say?"

"No. It isn't the same if you're the one to do it." I just wanted payback. I didn't want to get arrested.

"Well, it was good idea at least," Sandra said.

As I was about to answer, my phone dinged. I stealthily

pulled it out of my pocket, turning the screen's brightness down to avoid any death stares from the nearby moviegoers. My stomach dropped at the number of Twitter notifications.

"No way." I groaned, scrolling down the list. All the notifications were from a spoof account someone had made, @BirdbrainZach, who had tagged me in every tweet. The profile picture was a crudely photoshopped image of my sixth-grade yearbook photo. Me in that stupid striped shirt Mom had forced me to wear, only this time with a bird head. A pigeon, to be exact. Most of the feed was just GIFs and frozen stills from Samantha's video.

"Ouch." Sandra winced, looking over my shoulder. Her face glowed in the screen's bluish light. "You think it's Jeffrey?"

"It has to be. You think he'd waste an opportunity to humiliate me?" I pulled up @BirdbrainZach's follower list. "Look, he's even friended himself. Oh, no. He's friended Dominic too. I don't get it. This account's only a few hours old. How can he have more followers than me already?"

"Last time I checked, the video had over three hundred thousand views," Sandra said. "And that was this morning."

An idea formed in my head. If a spoof account could gain several hundred followers in just a few hours, how many followers had Samantha's Twitter and Instagram pages gotten from the video? Maybe this was the way I could impress Dominic and get back at Jeffrey, all at the same time.

I turned to Sandra. "You know the field trip on Monday?"

"What about it?" Her eyes widened. "Oh, no. You're not thinking..."

Smiling, I held up my phone. "Let's create another video. An even more viral one this time."

10

"ON SECOND THOUGHT, this is a horrible idea," I whispered to Sandra as the other kids in our class filed onto the bus. The vinyl seat squeaked beneath me as I leaned over her to peer out the window. "A horrible, horrible idea."

She elbowed me lightly in the side. "Don't whisper like that. You look suspicious."

"I can't help it. I'll give him five seconds before they throw him off the bus." I watched as Ash slipped into place at the back of the line. Sandra had taken him home from the theater, and he had spent the night hiding in her garage. She had gravely informed me that during those fifteen hours, he had inhaled three frozen pizzas, an entire carton of rocky road ice cream, and enough of her mom's famous potato llapingachos to feed a small army.

Who knew where all that food had gone? Except for his eerie amber eyes, Ash looked more or less like a normal seventh grader. From the way the other kids stared at him, I could already tell he was going to be our grade's most popular exchange student, if he managed to get past Mr. Clark at least.

While Ash had been cramming his face, I had spent all of Sunday night worrying about the video. At last, I had texted Samantha and asked her what it took to go viral. She had replied with LOL and told me I didn't really have what it took, but after enough pestering, she'd told me that there were three essential parts to making a viral video.

One: it had to evoke an emotion—humor, shock, anger. Two: the film couldn't be too choppy or too blurry, or else nobody would watch it. And three: you needed a following or at the very least, a way to spread it across the Internet. Samantha already had ten thousand followers, so for her, naturally, the video had gone viral. But unless I could hit all those checkmarks and find an audience for the video, I'd be out of luck.

First things first though, Ash needed to get on the bus. Gnawing my lower lip, I watched him go down the line. He was seven or eight people behind Dominic.

"Zach, don't look so worried," Sandra said, elbowing me gently in the side. "If Ash can convince the ice-cream man into giving him a free Drumstick, that takes some mad skills. He's going to be fine."

"Just wait until he opens his mouth. Then you'll see." I rolled my eyes. "Three racoons in a trench coat would make a more convincing seventh grader."

"If you say so, Mr. Negative."

"I'm not being negative, I'm just being realistic! Even if he manages to sneak on, there's still the chaperones. His name won't be on the list, and you know how much teachers love lists."

I was about to say more when Dominic reached the front of the line. As he climbed aboard, I watched him in the corner of my eye, too nervous to make eye contact directly.

There was something about Dominic's shaggy brown skater's cut and sky blue eyes that made him seem so *cool*. I couldn't explain it, except that the moment he'd stepped into our classroom for the first time, my breath had caught in my throat and my stomach fluttered with enough butterflies to fill an insectarium. I'd wanted to be his friend from day one. Just being close to him, sitting in the same row in class or sharing a lunch table, felt like it would be enough.

Except it was more than that. I'd only figured it out in the last year the reason I felt like I never fit in, or why all my dad's jokes about crushes felt like poking at a bruise. I didn't want to believe it at first. All I could imagine when I heard the word *gay* was the San Fran Pride photos I'd seen once—people decked in rainbows, glitter, and elaborate costumes.

I didn't like rainbows or face paint, so for a while, I tried convincing myself I couldn't possibly be gay. Except then I told Sandra my suspicions, and as my best friend of three years, she duly informed me that I could be gay, just the mopey, nerdy kind.

Dominic strode down the aisle, his hair hanging over his eyes the way I wished mine would, except mine usually ended sticking up in all directions. He was wearing a killer T-shirt with a howling wolf on the front, and I wondered if he'd like werewolf movies. Maybe I could tell him about *The Wolf Man* and ask him if he wanted to watch it. No, that one was too cheesy and not even scary. I needed to think of a cooler movie, not something so old that when it came out, my grandparents weren't even born yet!

As Dominic strolled down the bus aisle, I offered him a small smile. "Hey, Dom—" Mortifyingly, my voice chose that perfect moment to crack, and his name came out like a seagull's squawk.

He looked my way, frowning slightly in clear puzzlement at the obnoxious sound. I knew that when he smiled, a dimple would appear in his right cheek. I wished he'd smile back at me. Even a light, kindhearted chuckle would be worth my embarrassment.

I cleared my throat, praying my cheeks weren't as flushed as they felt. "Cool T-shirt. Do you like werewolf movies?"

He blinked. "Uh, no."

"Oh." Great, he didn't like them. I searched for something else to say. "Uh, you're on the baseball team, right? Did you watch, uh, that game with the Cubs and the, um, Packers, I think?"

He frowned. "The Packers play football."

Oh, no. He was going to think I was such a dork. Desperate to change the subject, I blurted out, "Are you looking forward to the zoo?"

"Yeah, I guess," Dominic said, flipping his hair out of his face. I sighed as he continued to the back of the bus and sank deeper into my seat, wishing I could turn invisible like Ash. It felt like there was an impassable rift between me and Dominic, like we existed in different worlds—me on planet dweeb and him on planet popular. I just hoped filming a viral video would land me in stardom.

"Zach," Sandra whispered, tugging on my sleeve.

Turning my attention back to the window, I held my breath as Ash reached the front of the line. Mr. Clark, an ex-Marine with a bumpy shaved head and the build of a brick wall, glanced down at his list and back again. Ash smiled and nodded. Mr. Clark frowned.

I frowned. "See, it's not working."

Mr. Clark sighed and waved Ash along.

"See?" Sandra smiled at me. "You're worrying over nothing."

As Ash came down the aisle, I waved my hand. "Hey, Ash, we're—ow!"

Something small and hard struck me on the forehead and made a tinkling sound as it hit the ground. I looked down and groaned. Not another penny.

Jeffrey sat a few rows down. With his twinkling blue eyes, pug nose, and cowlicked blond hair, he looked like what would happen if Dr. Frankenstein had brought one of my grandma's corny porcelain Hummel dolls to life—psychotic, ruddy cheeked, and grinning.

I'd heard people tell my mom before that if Naomi had been born back in the 1940s, her blond hair meant she'd be one of the lucky Jews, the ones who survived. Jeffrey, on the other hand? He'd almost definitely be a proud card-carrying member of the Hitler Youth.

Rubbing my forehead, I glowered at him.

"It's free money," he said with a laugh. "Why don't you pick it up, birdbrain?"

Sandra kept telling me I should tell a teacher, but the thing was the teachers knew it, and they didn't care. Last year, our PE teacher, Mr. Greyson, even told me to "man up," like I was supposed to challenge Jeffrey and his gang to a *Hunger Games*–style showdown. As far as I was concerned, a true man wouldn't let kids get bullied.

"On second thought, why film a viral video when we could just have Ash maul him?" I muttered as Jeffrey turned back ahead.

"It could be worse," Sandra said. "It could be boogers."

"No, those are too precious to Jeffrey. He needs to save them for his after-school snacks."

Ash strolled over and took the empty seat across from us. He leaned down and picked up the penny, riffling it over his knuckles in a blur before catching it in one hand.

"You will both be pleased to know, I am very much a master in the art of revenge." Excitement sparked in his golden eyes, and when he smiled, his teeth were sharper than they should've been. "Tell me all that he's done to you, Zach. I'll devise the perfect way to pay him back tenfold."

"I appreciate the offer," I said, "but I'm not looking to become an accessory to murder."

"I'm not suggesting you kill him. Simply an eye for an eye, with a little extra."

"No blinding him either," I said, appalled. "This isn't the Middle Ages, Ash. People go to jail for those things, and besides, I may like horror movies, but I have no intention of becoming a supervillain. I'll leave that to you."

"So, you are giving me permission—"

"No!" Sandra and I said in unison.

Ash sighed heavily. "Ah, you humans. You're seldom fun."

"You want fun? Just wait until the zoo." I glared at the back of Jeffrey's head. "After today, he won't be able to look at a rotisserie chicken without bursting into tears."

Sandra cocked her head, studying me with a sly smile. From the gleam in her brown eyes, I could tell the ring's appeal was growing on her. "What exactly do you have in mind?"

"We're going to pull an Alfred Hitchcock on him." I reached into my pocket, tightening my fingers around the ring. *"The Birds."*

11

"CLOSED?!" I GAWKED in disbelief at the sign hanging from the birdhouse's door. Through the screen mesh, I caught a glimpse of the tropical parrots perched in the trees. My one chance at revenge, gone. "How can they be closed?"

"Sorry, Zach," Mr. Clark said, patting me on the head. Sandra and I had the bad luck of being paired off with his group for the trip. Now I had the added bonus of worrying that whatever mayhem I used the ring for, Mr. Clark would use his Marine skills to karate chop it into submission.

"What's the matter, birdbrain?" Jeffrey asked, shoving me in the shoulder. "Sad you can't be pooped on again?"

I glared at his retreating figure. Plan B. If I wasn't able to re-create iconic scenes from *The Birds*, at the very least I needed to expose him to the true horrors of the petting zoo. I hoped Jeffrey liked being crushed in a stampede of billy goats and ponies.

"Maybe we should just throw him into the alligator pond," Ash said merrily, tagging alongside me. Somehow, he had convinced Mr. Clark that, despite not being on the list, he had been assigned to our group.

"Shouldn't you be the one coming to my defense?" I asked. "You know, instead of relying upon alligators to do it?"

"I'm the guardian of the ring, not the guardian of its temporary owner," he said. "Besides, you haven't asked me to. I would be more than happy to lend you my help, if you just asked."

"I'm a little afraid of what you mean by your *help*," I said.

"Not to mention what it might cost," Sandra added warily, always on the lookout for my eternal soul.

Ahead, Jeffrey merged with Dominic's friend circle. They were with four other boys who I knew by name but wasn't close to. I wish I could find a way to become part of Dominic's group, to prove to them that I was worthy.

As I watched, Jeffrey leaned over and whispered something in Dominic's ear. Dominic laughed, his blue eyes sparkling with amusement. A twinge of resentment burrowed deep inside me. I was sure that I could tell a much funnier joke than what Jeffrey just said.

Mr. Clark clapped his hands. "Okay, huddle up. I don't know about you, but I'm ready for some grub. Why don't we take a break at the food court, and then we'll figure out what to do after that? We're supposed to meet up at one o'clock for a visit to the veterinary clinic here, but aside from that, what were you kids wanting to see?"

Sandra raised her hand. "Dolphins."

"Wolves and bears," Dominic said.

"I fully agree with the mop-headed child," Ash called out, earning a disgruntled look from Dominic. "Take us to the deadly animals."

"No, lizards!" Jeffrey said, apparently eager to be reunited with his own kind.

"How about the petting zoo?" I said lamely, earning a few mocking laughs. Sandra lifted her eyebrows. I turned to her once the others were out of earshot. "It's the only place we'll actually have access to the animals. We can't really scare Jeffrey from behind glass."

"You have a point," she admitted. "But I don't think he'll be traumatized by a cuteness overload."

"Any better ideas?"

"Yeah, getting a veggie burger." She ran a hand through her dark hair. "We still have all day. Let's plot over lunch."

I sighed as she followed after the others. I guessed even evil masterminds needed to eat.

"Aren't you coming?" Sandra asked, glancing back at me.

"In a minute. I want to try out the ring where no one can hear me."

"You'll get in trouble if you wander off."

"I'll catch up, don't worry." I looked past her. Ash was making a beeline for the pizza stand. "Can you keep an eye on him? He's like a puppy. If he keeps running off like this, we'll have to invest in a leash."

She rolled her eyes. "Fine, but I call dibs on the ring after lunch."

"It's all yours."

As she ran after Ash, I followed the signs back to the lion enclosure. Jeffrey and the others were nowhere in sight, but I glanced around just to be sure. Slipping my finger through the ring, I leaned over the railing. Down below, it was a fifteen-foot drop to a grass-dappled pen. The closest lion was thirty feet away, and any sound it made was lost beneath the mindless chatter of the birds perched in the branches overhead.

"Hey, lions," I called.

The king ignored me, but a lioness padded over in interest.

"Hey there." I grinned. "What's your name?"

Her wide pink tongue drew a line over her muzzle. "Come closer, and I'll tell you, human."

The lioness's greenish-gold eyes gleamed in the sun. She smiled, but in the way our neighbor's cat smiled after delivering headless mice to our doorstep—a white crest of fangs speckled with saliva.

"Uh, actually, I think I'll stay up here," I said, and was about to say more when someone snatched the ring from my hand. I swiveled around to find Jeffrey grinning at me.

"Nice jewelry, birdbrain. Do you wear your mom's makeup, too?"

"Give that back!" I made a grab for it. Jeffrey shoved me in the chest, holding the ring high above my head. Ugh, why was he so big? Did his ancestors marry ogres or something, or did being evil just give you all the perks in life?

"Or what? What are you going to do?" He stepped back and put the ring on his own finger. Not good. This was so not good.

"You know, maybe I should just pitch this piece of crap into the lion pit."

I swallowed hard. "I don't think that's a good idea."

"Yeah?" He leaned over the railing, waving the ring in the air. "Hey, lions! You want this?"

"I mean it. It might—" I searched desperately for an excuse. "It might give them indigestion."

The beasts circled below. They must have had some choice words for Jeffrey because his eyes nearly popped out of his head and his face paled to the color of cottage cheese. He stared down in slack-jawed shock. "Did you hear that? They just—"

A passing man reached over and nonchalantly plucked the ring from Jeffrey's fingers. "You shouldn't take things that don't belong to you, kid."

I sighed in relief. "Thanks. That's mine."

The man smiled. Dressed in a white polo shirt and khakis, with his thick brown hair brushed back from his face, he looked like an escapee from a Hallmark holiday movie. His green eyes even twinkled. "Oh really?"

"Yeah, really."

Cocking his head, he held the signet ring to the light, admiring the way the sunlight gleamed over the polished garnets set along the seal's edge. "Magnificent. The craftsmanship is superb. Is it an antique?"

In the corner of my eye, I watched Jeffrey shift uneasily, retreating to the edge of the path. "It's just something I bought at a flea market for my mom. Can I have it back now, please?"

"Here." The man held out his hand.

As I reached for the ring, his other hand closed around my shirt collar. He drove me against the pit's railing, hard enough that pain shot down my back and my teeth rattled.

"Hey, let go of me!" I tried to worm out from his grasp, but he was too strong. Keeping an iron grip on my collar, he raised me higher until my butt brushed against the top of the railing.

Uh-oh.

As Jeffrey turned and bolted, the man flashed me a Hollywood-bright grin. "Sorry, kiddo. How's about you say we give this ring a test-drive?"

Desperately, I clawed at his neck and face. My fingers snagged the gold necklace he wore, but the chain broke free in my hands as he pushed me over the edge.

12

THE BLUE SKY spun overhead in a nauseating blur, like I'd taken a turn on a carnival ride, only with none of the fun. Then, just as quickly, the fall ended. I slammed into the dirt, gasping for breath. For a long moment, I could only lie there, stunned senseless. So, this was how it felt when we launched Naomi's old Bratz dolls in homemade catapults.

"Consider him my gift to you," the man called cheerfully, peering over the railing. "Gobble up, boys."

A low growl rose ahead. Slowly, I hoisted myself onto my hands and knees, wincing at the pain in my side.

Three lions slunk closer, their muscles rippling beneath their sleek coats. One lioness bared her teeth and growled low in her throat, her teeth glistening in the sunlight.

"You don't have to do this," I pleaded, praying that the ring had left me with some residue of power. "I really don't taste good. And I'm friends with Ashmedai. You don't want to piss off the king of demons, do you?"

The king of the pride was a lion so muscular that it looked like he bench-pressed in his free time and ate steroids for breakfast. He crouched down, body tensing.

Why wasn't anyone coming to help me? Were the zookeepers snoozing on the job?

People leaned over the railing, yelling and pointing at me, some even waving their families over as if I was part of the exhibit. A few of the real sick ones had their phones out and were filming.

As I backed away from the lions, sirens blared. In the distance, a wolf howled, and tropical birds shrieked up a fury, but nothing was as loud as the pounding of my own heart or the blood rushing through my ears.

"Ash!" I yelled, searching for his face among the observers. Where was he? For the supposed guardian of the ring, he was doing an awfully poor job of keeping an eye on it!

As I opened my mouth to shout his name once more, the largest of the lions pounced forward. I leaped out of the way. Dirt spewed across my leg as the cat landed mere inches from where I had been standing.

My mom had always warned me that if I came across coyotes or a mountain lion in the wild, it was important to stand my ground and not run, because when you ran, it activated the beast's killer instincts. I had a feeling that falling into a zoo exhibit put that prey drive into full throttle.

"Stay back!" I shouted, waving my arms around to seem larger that I really was. The lion prowled forward, undeterred.

If waving my arms around did anything, it simply upgraded my status from a Kid's Meal to a Big Mac in the creature's eyes.

The two lionesses circled, licking their chops. Why couldn't I have gotten hooked on *National Geographic* documentaries when I had the chance? I knew how to survive a dozen horror film encounters, but wild beasts weren't exactly on my doomsday itinerary.

The king lion crouched down, preparing to leap. As he lunged forward, a silver blur whizzed through the air. Dirt spewed across the clearing as a metal rod embedded itself in the soil. It was the same sign that had warned visitors not to lean over the railings, one end broken into a jagged point.

The lion leaped back and resumed his prowl, a wary glint in his eyes. I wrenched the pole from the ground. Better than trying to face the wildcats down in a fistfight.

Seconds later, Ash landed beside me. I hadn't seen him vault off the railing, but I heard the shocked and appalled cries of the people watching. He somehow had the sense to remain in human form, but there was something immediately unnatural in the way he rose to his feet, unwavering, after a fifteen-foot drop.

"I will say this day has proved to be much more interesting than I expected," he said cheerfully, apparently unconcerned with the possibility of becoming lion chow.

"Where were you?" I demanded, then winced at the sharp pain in my side.

"Sandra and I were hunting down some more of that delicious pizza. You should've waited until I came back. I'm appalled that you would do this without me, Zach. Back in my day, this was considered peak Roman entertainment."

"Ash, this isn't some game—" I leaped back as the lion pounced at me, raising the pole like a club. With a single swing of his paw, the beast swatted away the pole as though it were nothing more than a sippy straw. I retreated until my back pressed against the cement wall of the enclosure.

"If I may," Ash said, stepping past me. He confronted the big cats with a smile, his golden eyes gleaming unnaturally in the sunlight. The two lionesses backed away, but the lion crouched, its muscles straining beneath its velvety pelt.

Ash murmured softly, his voice rising and falling around strange syllables. I couldn't catch what he was saying, only that it was a language I didn't understand, but one that felt even older than our prayers.

"What are you saying?" I whispered.

He raised a finger to shush me. "I'm negotiating."

"Negotiating what?"

"Your life."

The king lion growled deep in his throat, baring his teeth as he stepped even closer.

Ash winced. "Not good."

"What did he say?!"

"Plan two." As the lion lunged at us, Ash seized me around the waist and launched into the air.

13

THE GROUND GAVE way beneath me in an instant. We surged upward in a flurry of black feathers, going so fast that I couldn't tell whether the scream in my ears was coming from my own mouth or if it was just the sound of the wind whistling through Ash's wings. Waves of cold air thrashed against me as Ash's wings unfurled, sending us spiraling high above the zoo until the people and animals alike were reduced to ants.

Not good. Not good. I clung to him, scrambling for a hold.

"Don't you dare drop me!" I shouted, and squeezed my eyes shut. "Get us down now. I hate heights. I'm going to be sick."

The threat of barfing did it. A sudden plunge in altitude sent us plummeting ten feet in an instant, coming dangerously close to skewering ourselves on the branches of the nearby trees. Ash managed to flap his wings before we were reduced to human shish kebabs, slowing our fall to a smooth, slow descent. We touched down on solid ground.

"For someone who boasts about their limitless power, you could've made that landing a bit smoother," I croaked as he let go of me.

"It's been a good three hundred years since I've had to carry a passenger," he said, huffing. His wings dissolved into smoke, wisping away to nothing in a matter of seconds. "Just be grateful I didn't leave you for the lions."

"This isn't good," I said breathlessly, grasping on to a tree until the world stopped spinning. "Not good at all. This isn't the Middle Ages, Ash. People just don't go flying around anymore. Now we'll get the FBI sicced on us. They'll dissect you, Ash."

"Calm down, Zechariah."

"It's Zach," I reminded him for the billionth time.

"Fine, Zach. Take a deep breath. Back in the day, I started a few more witch hunts than I intended, so I know how worked up you humans get when you see evidence of the divine. Don't worry, nobody saw us."

"But we flew right past them!"

He laughed. "If you don't believe me, look down at yourself."

I lowered my gaze. My hands were as see-through as dragonfly wings. Even my clothing had become transparent. It terrified me not being able to see myself. I reached down to reassure myself that my body was still there, grasping at my chest until I felt my cotton shirt beneath my hands, and below that, the pounding beat of my heart. Slowly, I released my held breath.

"See?" He smiled. "Even the lowliest of shedim is capable of invisibility. You think I, the king of demons, would be incapable of such a feat? Don't make me laugh."

"I hate to break it to you, Ash, but you're not invisible." I fought to keep my voice steady. He might have been able to turn me invisible, but apparently his powers had fluked.

He scoffed. "Do you truly underestimate me so? The only reason you can see me is because I allow it."

"But the cameras," I said weakly. "People had their phones out."

"As I said before, relax. Humans can scarcely tolerate looking upon the true face of the divine, and I doubt those things you call cameras are any exception."

"I wouldn't be so sure of that."

As he combed the leaves out of his hair, I settled back against the trunk and watched as the color slowly began to return to my hands.

"So, care to explain how you ended up in the lion den?" he asked.

"Some guy pushed me in there."

"What did you do?"

I sputtered. "Nothing! He stole the ring."

Ash froze. "What did you say?"

"I don't know who he was. He just took it and then pushed me in."

"And you let him?" Ash's voice rose in rage, his eyes flashing dangerously.

"It's not my fault! Jeffrey grabbed the ring from me, and then this man took it from Jeffrey. He seemed to know what it was. How could he have known?"

Ash took a deep breath, and the unnatural radiance of his eyes died into a faint smolder. "Tell me, what did he look like?"

"He just looked like a regular person. Like an actor or something."

"An actor?"

"You know, the kind of actor who plays the dad in the movies. Tanned, white teeth, big smile. You follow?"

He glowered at me. "No, I don't follow."

"You aren't going to disappear or anything, right? Now that the ring is gone?"

"No. It can awaken shedim, but it cannot summon them when they're already awake. The greatest danger would be if the thief tried to..." He trailed off.

"Try to what?"

"Use it on me. To compel me." Ash looked away, an embarrassed blush spreading across his cheeks. "But he would have to be close for that, and he'd have to know what to do."

"So it *can* control you!"

"Only because my—" His jaw snapped shut, and he narrowed his eyes. "Forget it."

"Let's go back to the lion exhibit. Maybe he's still hanging around."

We hurried in the direction of the lion pit. By now, the crowd was beginning to fade. Considering my disappearing act, I was pretty sure that I had landed a new place at the top of YouTube's most viral videos. This wasn't what I'd meant when I told Sandra, *Let's film another video.* My parents were going to be so pissed. If they found out, they'd chew me out so badly, it'd make being devoured by lions look like a walk through the park.

"They just disappeared!" a woman was telling a small squadron of zookeepers, waving her phone frantically in the air. "Two boys. I swear, they were in the pit, just ask anyone."

"My phone is broken," a man howled in despair. Other unlucky iPhone owners wandered around with dazed looks, cradling their own black-screened phones like shell-shocked soldiers.

Keeping my head down, I edged past the pair. Hopefully, Mr. Clark was too busy fueling his imposing physique with hotdogs and burgers to have noticed Ash and me gone.

Plenty of people still lingered around the lion pit, likely itching to see if we would come back for an encore.

"It has to be some sort of Hollywood prank," a teenage girl said. "It's probably part of a reality TV show."

The one good thing about living in California was that everything that happened felt a little fake. Even out here in San Pancras, you couldn't go to a restaurant without risking being mauled by hordes of Instagram influencers photographing their untouched food. And I couldn't count the number of times we had ended up snared in a traffic jam because a horde of paparazzi was following after celebrities like a pack of slobbering dogs. Thank God for Hollywood.

By the time we reached the lion pit, we were fully visible. I expected at any moment someone to shout out, "Look, there they are!" But nobody even glanced in our direction.

"Do you see him?" Ash asked, scanning the remaining observers.

I shook my head. "He must've left."

At the railing, Ash leaned down and picked something from the ground. He opened his hand to reveal a thick chain coiled around his fingers, a gold pendant swinging like a pendulum. I recognized it as the necklace the man at the zoo had worn, that I'd torn off during our struggle.

"Here." He tossed it to me.

I caught the necklace in my cupped hands and turned it over. The disc was engraved with a snake encircling a lit torch, in the process of consuming its own tail.

"The man who attacked you, did he drop this?" Ash asked.

"He was wearing it," I said.

"Do you recognize this symbol?"

I shook my head.

He frowned. "It's familiar... I can't remember where or when I saw it last, but...yeah, it's familiar."

"Did it have something to do with Solomon?"

"No, this was later." His gaze clouded over. "Much, much later. A small stone cottage along the river. The family offered me shavfka and peppers stuffed with rice."

"When was that, and where?"

"I don't remember. It's all just a blur to me."

"What about the ring? Can you sense it?"

Ash closed his eyes, concentrating. A slight breeze picked up around his feet, scattering the dead leaves and litter. I could feel the change in the air, the subtle shift of his strange and mystical gravity. Just as quickly, the wind died down and he sagged against the railing, his face blanched to an unhealthy yellowish tone.

"I don't feel so good," he groaned, pressing his hand over his mouth. I stepped back quickly. I had watched *The Exorcist* enough times to know that demon puke was a nightmare to get out of clothes.

"What's the matter?" I asked. "Is it something to do with the ring or the pendant?"

"Pizza," he said. "I never should've flown after eating four slices of pizza."

I guessed even demons could have upset stomachs. Luckily, instead of projectile vomiting on everything within a six-foot radius, he simply plopped down on the grass and cradled his face in his hands.

"Something is wrong with me," he whispered, and I realized he didn't just mean his upset stomach. "I can't feel it. The ring. I can't feel it anymore. My powers. There's something wrong with me."

"What kind of pizza did you eat?" Could the man have slipped something into Ash's food, some magical herb or potion strong enough to knock out his powers?

Ash groaned, lowering his hands to his stomach. "The brown kind."

"The brown kind?! Ash, I'm pretty sure pizza doesn't come in brown, unless you dug it out of a trash can." An awful thought occurred to me. "Oh, please tell me you didn't do that."

"No, I mean the stripes on it. The salty brown stripes."

"Wait, do you mean anchovies?"

He just groaned in answer.

I remembered what he had said on the first night about not eating either birds or fish. "Ash, are you allergic to fish?"

He cracked open one eye—the golden radiance surrounding his iris had diminished to a dying ember, growing duller by the moment. "Why does it matter?"

"Anchovies are fish, Ash!" I said, and was about to say more when the heavy clomp of footsteps came up behind me.

"Zach Darlington!" a voice barked.

14

I TURNED TO find Mr. Clark striding toward us, his face turning so red, it looked as if a ripe tomato had been transplanted onto his thick, veiny neck. "We've been looking all over for you. I told you not to wander off on your own. Didn't you hear? Some kid just fell into an enclosure!"

I fumbled for a response. "Sorry, Mr. Clark. Ash was feeling sick, so I was trying to help him find a bathroom."

Mr. Clark turned to Ash as if only just recalling his presence. He furrowed his bushy brows. "What's the matter?"

"Too much pizza," Ash croaked, and then burped. I groaned.

"You might want to step back," I warned Mr. Clark as Ash staggered to his feet, his face looking greener by the moment. I searched for a suitable shield in case he started barfing, but the only thing Ash cast my way was a withering look.

"I'm fine," Ash said, drawing in a shallow breath. "I'm sorry. It was my fault."

Mr. Clark shook his head, running a hand over the bumpy planes of his skull. "In any case, get back to the bus. The rest of the field trip's been cancelled. There's something weird going on with the animals today. They're all acting up."

With a glance back at the lion pit, I followed after Mr. Clark. By the time we returned to the bus, everyone had heard about the two kids who'd fallen into the lion exhibit, although only Jeffrey seemed to know what had happened. The moment his eyes landed on me, they bugged out of his skull, and his face paled by a few shades. It dawned on me that he hadn't even told Mr. Clark about what happened. He had probably been hoping I'd become lion food first.

Sandra rushed over to us. "What happened? Zach, please tell me you weren't the one who—"

I shook my head. "Later. Something's happened. The ring is gone."

"Gone?!"

"The ogre over there stole it—" i nodded in Jeffrey's direction "—and then someone took it from him. A grown-up."

Once we were on the bus, I whispered to her how the ring had gotten snatched and our short but eventful flight. She listened gravely, pausing only to offer Ash her water bottle when he let out an especially pitiful groan.

We had the back of the bus to ourselves. The moment Ash had staggered aboard and Mr. Clark had handed him the tiny trash can behind the driver's seat, the other students had quickly vacated the last three rows to escape the splash zone.

"Are you sure you were invisible?" she asked. "Because I have a feeling this is how the movie *E.T.* started."

"Relax, no one is getting dissected," I said. "I'm pretty sure Ash ruined five thousand dollars' worth of iPhones just by transforming."

"No way," she said.

I nodded.

"Do you think they'll know it's you?" she asked. "I mean, before he used his powers. Could the cameras have picked it up?"

"I don't know," I admitted. "Honestly, I think the most important thing right now is getting the ring back. The guy who took it, he seemed to know what it was capable of."

"How could he have known?"

A bad feeling brewed in the pit of my stomach. It was too much of a coincidence that the ring thief had just happened to be at the zoo at the perfect time, except now that I thought about it, I was pretty sure I'd seen him earlier in the day too. Lurking through the monkey house, speaking into his Bluetooth. Lingering by the buses, his gaze following us.

With his perfectly coiffed brown hair and Hollywood-bright smile, he hadn't seemed like your typical creep, so he had faded into the background. At the very least, he should have brought his Free Candy sign so that we'd know to steer clear of him.

"There's only one explanation," I said. "He watched Samantha's video and came here looking for me. He knows who I am, and he knows what the ring is capable of."

By the time school let out and Sandra's mom picked us up, the multiple videos that flooded the Internet of our narrow brush with death quickly became more viral than Samantha's seagull video. We sat on Sandra's bed, watching them on her laptop. Most of the videos were shaky and blurry, shot from above at awkward angles. The two boys in the lion pit could've been anyone. I doubted even my own parents would recognize me.

In all of the videos, the moment Ash had transformed, the scene had been reduced to a streak of light and shadow. The blur that surged skyward out of frame could've been a dark-winged demon, but most commenters thought it was a pigeon or even a trick of the light. The rest wondered if it was a Hollywood stunt for advertising an upcoming fantasy film.

"What did I tell you?" Ash said with an amused huff as I clicked on the next video. "Even your petty human devices are incapable of gazing upon the true might of the divine."

"Last time I checked, you were pretty sure I had captured a ghost inside of my smartphone," I said dryly.

"A sheyd," he corrected. "One of the weaker ones, of course. I'd never be so foolish as to allow myself to be trapped in such an unrefined vessel."

"Do you see the man in any of these videos?" Sandra asked, returning from the kitchen with a bowl of microwave popcorn, which she dutifully gave to Ash.

"No sign of him," I said.

"So, the only clue we have is the necklace. Great."

I slipped the pendant from my pocket. The sunlight filtering through the window gleamed across the coiled serpent engraved on the disc's face. When I tilted the pendant around in my palm so that it caught the light, the snake appeared to writhe.

"There has to be a way to figure out what that symbol

means," Sandra said. "Or at the very least where the pendant came from."

I gave it some thought. "Maybe my cousin Samantha knows something. She's the one who filmed the birdnado video, so the ring thief could've reached out to her first."

"That settles it then," Ash proclaimed from his perch atop Sandra's desk. He jumped down, popcorn still in hand. "Take me to her."

15

MY AUNT AND uncle lived in the south end of San Pancras, on a street of condos overlooking the bay. When I knocked on the door, my aunt answered with a bemused smile. "Oh, Zach, what are you doing here? Are these your friends?"

"Yeah, this is Sandra and Ash." I offered my sweetest smile. "Is Samantha home?"

"She's in her bedroom, but why do you ask?"

"No time to explain," I said, hurrying down the hall.

The birdnado video might've gone viral, but it wasn't what got Samantha her ten-thousand-strong following. She also designed costumes and was a makeup artist, but sadly not the kind that made actors look like monsters.

Last time I visited, she had rigged her bedroom up as her Instagram studio, complete with a green screen and movie lights. When I entered, she was sitting at her makeup desk, except now the only thing that lay in front of her was a sprawl of papers. She glanced up as I came near and frowned.

"Zach, what are you doing here? I'm in the middle of homework. And you brought…friends?" She arched an eyebrow.

"It's about your video, the one you filmed at Grandma's house."

Sighing, she set aside her bulky textbook. Her blond hair spread in a curtain behind her, so long it nearly touched the seat of her rolling chair. "Look, I didn't expect it to go viral like that. Why? Are kids at school giving you trouble?"

"It's actually about an adult," Sandra cut in.

Samantha furrowed her brow. "An adult?"

"We were just wondering if any adults had contacted you about the video," Sandra said carefully. "You know, like fans."

"Well, now that you mention it, there was a weird message," she said. "I already deleted it actually."

"What sort of message?" Ash asked.

"It was just one of those Renaissance Fair guys, I think. You know, the Dungeons & Dragons type."

D&D didn't exactly mix with polo shirts and radioactively white smiles, but what did I know? Maybe it was still the same guy.

"What do you mean?" I asked.

Samantha rolled her eyes. "Well, he called himself a knight and said he hailed from an ancient order. Then he asked about a magic ring."

I gulped, exchanging a look with Sandra and Ash. That had to be it.

"I get messages like that all the time. You just ignore them or report them. You don't engage. But really, what's this all about?" Her ice-blue eyes narrowed, studying me like I was one of her algebra equations. "Wait. Don't tell me he tried messaging you, too?"

Deciding it was better not to involve another member of my family in this mess, I shook my head. "It's nothing. We'll let you get back to your homework. Thanks for your help, Sam."

16

OUTSIDE, I SQUINTED against the sun's white glare, the sudden change in temperature making my cheeks prickle. Even the warmth of the sun beating down on us couldn't thaw the chill in my veins.

"He called himself a knight," I said. "So, what? We're dealing with Gandalf here?"

"Gandalf is a wizard," Sandra informed me. "And from the sound of it, there's more than one person involved. It's not just that weirdo. It's a group of them."

A group of them. Suddenly, it dawned on me that the guy from the zoo had been wearing a polo shirt just like the creepy park woman, with the same sewed-on badge. And hadn't the older lady at the theater, the one I thought was watching us, also been wearing a polo beneath her pink knit cardigan? It had been too dark to get a good look at her, but I could've sworn she'd had one on too.

"If we're dealing with some sort of secret organization, there's only one person who can help us," Sandra declared, flipping down her bike's kickstand. With a grin, she hopped onto her bike. "Follow me."

I barely had enough time to climb on my bike before Ash zipped past on the spare he'd borrowed from Sandra, pedaling almost as erratically as he flew. It was a good thing none of us could drive yet, because if he got behind the wheel of a car, he'd probably mow down pedestrians at every crosswalk.

The sun beat down on us, and a steady burn spread through my calves. I tried to focus on the road ahead, flexing and tightening my fingers around the foam handlebar sleeves. But all I could think about was the man from the zoo, and how he had looked so normal. My mom and dad always warned Naomi and me that there were bad people in the world, but I'd always envisioned retro horror movie villains, not someone who looked open and friendly, like a dad from a sitcom.

We turned off the main road, through a neighborhood of identical stucco houses, then reached an area I had only seen in passing. Soon we stopped at a strip mall whose walls were painted the color of Pepto-Bismol. Only a few of the shops had their Open signs on—a nail salon and the barbershop right next to it, a psychic advertising palm readings for five dollars a pop, and a comics and game store.

"I don't think a psychic is going to be able to help us," I told Sandra as she came to a stop along the sidewalk.

"That's not why I brought us here," she said as we locked our bikes up at the rack out front.

"I don't think getting a manicure will either."

She rolled her eyes, striding across the blacktop. "You're hopeless. Come on."

As we stepped into the comic shop, the bells above the door chimed. Shelves held colorful boxes and books, and more comics and rare collectibles were arranged in display cases behind glass. My eye was drawn to a vintage *Dracula* poster hanging on the wall in a Plexiglas frame, but I resisted the impulse to make a beeline for it and dutifully followed Sandra deeper into the store.

The cashier was a teenage boy with a shock of carrot-red hair that looked like it'd destroyed even more combs than mine. As we went up to the counter, he blinked slowly, lizard-like, and turned the page of the *Sandman* comic spread over the cash register.

"Is Carmen here?" Sandra asked.

Rubbing a mole on his cheek, he jerked his chin to the back of the shop. "On break."

"Who's Carmen?" Ash asked as he followed Sandra and me deeper into the store.

"*My* cousin," she said triumphantly.

"I hope she's able to help us more than mine," I added, earning an eye roll.

Turning back ahead, I scanned the shelves. I couldn't believe that I hadn't been in the store before, not when it had an entire section dedicated to vintage scary classics like *Tales from the Crypt* and *Adventures into the Unknown*. I craned my head to get a better luck at the stacks across the store. Was that a collector's edition of *30 Days of Night*?

Sandra slapped my hand. I turned to her, rubbing my knuckles in indignation.

"What was that for?"

She thrust a finger in my face. "Don't think I don't see you eyeing that. Focus, Zach."

Geez, she was almost as bad as our second-period science teacher, Mrs. Hill, who would confiscate my notebook each time she caught me doodling between assignments. Worse, she was the kind of sadistic teacher who marked points down on tests if I drew in the margins.

"Hey, Ash, that's you," I said as we passed a rack of *Hellboy* comics, although I was pretty sure that the superhero was only half-demon. Come to think of it, if Hellboy could be a superhero, then it wasn't too much of a stretch to think that the king of demons himself could be good for once—especially after what my mom had told me about the differences between shedim like Ash and your typical Hollywood demons.

"I assure you, human, my true form is far more magnificent than that...thing," Ash said, wrinkling his nose.

"If it's so impressive, why don't you just show us?" Sandra asked.

Ash smirked. "Unfortunately, humans like you are seldom able to gaze upon the divine and live to tell the tale."

Okay, so maybe he wasn't a superhero after all.

Voices filtered from deeper into the store. In the back room lined with shelves of video games and board games, a blue-haired teenager leaned over an old pinball machine, working the levers and buttons.

Glancing at the score on the screen, my mouth came unhinged. No way, how could you even get a million points in this game?

"Carmen—" Sandra began, and the girl made *neh-eh* sounds deep in her throat, that sounded a lot like what you'd make if your dog was making a beeline for your birthday cake.

"Not a word," Carmen said, her dark eyes riveted to the screen. The game's neon lights danced across her round glasses and turned her peacock-blue hair practically fluorescent. If Sandra got her love of the color black from her older brother, then she must've gotten her great taste from Carmen, because when the girl turned around, her shirt was emblazoned with the characters from *Kingdom Hearts III*, Sandra's favorite video game.

"Yes, 1,560,000," Carmen crowed, pumping her fist in the air. Tipping her glasses up the bridge of her nose again, she smiled at us. "Sandra, what are you doing here? Oh, are these your friends from school?"

"Yeah, this is my best friend, Zach, and our new friend, Ash."

"Nice to meet you," I said.

"Ash like in Pokémon?" Carmen asked, and although he couldn't possibly have known about Pokémon, he scoffed as though offended at sharing the name with a measly mortal.

"Ash is in Ashmedai, king of demons," he declared.

Carmen nodded, still smiling, although it was clear she had absolutely no idea what he was talking about. Deciding that it would be good idea to butt in before he ended up blowing up on her for not knowing to call him Your Highness, I cleared my throat. "Sandra thinks that you can help us with…"

"Trying to figure out what a weird occult symbol means," Sandra said, before turning to me. "Carmen loves the spooky stuff too, Zach. She knows all about cryptids, strange societies, and the really obscure hauntings."

Carmen cocked her head, giving it some thought. "Well, I guess I can give it a shot. Do you have a picture?"

"Something even better." I took the pendant from my pocket and passed it over to her.

Frowning, she turned it around in her hands.

"Where'd you get this?" Carmen asked, glancing up.

"Uh, the flea market."

"This symbol of a snake eating its tail is called an Ouroboros. It's an ancient symbol for eternity."

"What about the torch?" I asked.

"Well, that's an easy one." Carmen chuckled. "A torch for knowledge or insight. For illuminating the darkness of the unknown. It could even be a symbol for purification, with the flame representing cleansing. And the snake also represents rebirth on its own, or could even be a reference to the Garden of Eden. Whatever these symbols stand for, it shouldn't be hard to figure out more."

"Knights," I blurted out, earning a befuddled look. "It's a group. It's called the Knights, or something with Knights in it."

"Well, that definitely sounds like it would match a secret society." Carmen frowned. "But I thought you said you got this at a flea market, so how do you know it belongs to a group?"

"Uh, lucky guess?"

"Don't lie to me, Zach. I know a liar when I see one." She pointed an accusatory finger at me.

I groaned. "It's too hard to explain."

"Carmen, can you just help us figure out what it means?" Sandra asked, crossing her arms.

"Oh, fine. Keep it a secret then." Carmen handed the pendant back to me and pulled out a chair at the table. "I still have a bit of time left on my break. Sit down, let me just grab my laptop from the back room."

We sat down, waiting tensely as she retreated deeper into the store.

"Why didn't you tell me you had such a cool cousin?" I asked Sandra.

"You never asked."

"Can we trade?"

Rolling her eyes, Sandra shoved me lightly in the shoulder. "You wish."

Carmen returned a few minutes later with her laptop case and a plastic bag.

"Hope you don't mind if I eat too," Carmen said, pulling out a wrapped sub and a bag of chips. The moment she unwrapped her sandwich, my mouth puckered involuntarily at the fishy odor that struck me in an instant. Dear god, it reeked like tuna that had been left a week in a hot dumpster.

Across the table, Ash shriveled back, his face going green

in an instant. He pressed a hand over his nose, giving Carmen such a glare that it should have struck her dead, or at least ruined her appetite. Instead, she took a heaping bite of the sandwich, nearly groaning in ecstasy as she chewed.

"You guys have to try this," she said, once she had washed down the mouthful of that unholy atrocity with a glug of her pineapple energy drink. "It's from the sandwich place across the street."

"What is it?" I asked, resisting the impulse to projectile vomit across the room.

"Tuna melt." She took another bite. "They have this special sauce they use. It's absolutely amazing."

I exchanged a look with Sandra, who shrugged her shoulders and pretended to pinch her nose the moment Carmen looked away.

As far as my nose was concerned, the sandwich shop's employees probably whipped together the secret sauce from whatever they could scrape out from beneath the counters and grill each week. I hadn't smelled anything this nasty since my mom had tried making her great-grandmother's gefilte fish recipe one summer.

I hoped Carmen would keep eating so that the only thing we'd have to worry about was the smell of her breath, but instead she placed the sub on my side of the table and turned her attention back to her laptop. Discreetly, I shifted the sub away from me. As the offensive sandwich slid toward Ash, he glowered at me and pushed it back, being careful to only touch the paper wrapping she used as her plate.

"So, let's see what we have here," Carmen said, typing into her computer. Without looking away, she reached down, groping for her sandwich. If she noticed how its location had moved, she showed no sign of it, and simply took another heaping bite. I hoped that the military would not discover the secret tuna recipe. Otherwise I had no doubt that it would end up in their arsenal in only a matter of time.

"You might also want to type in 'demon' and 'ring of Solomon,'" I added helpfully.

"That's a bit specific," Carmen said, glancing up with a frown. "Want to start telling me where you got this necklace for real?"

"Alcántara," Ash said quietly, and I looked across the table to find him staring hollowly at his feet, as though he was looking at something far behind him. "I remember now. The last time I saw that symbol was in Alcántara."

"That sounds Spanish," Carmen said. "Was that somewhere here in California?"

He shook his head. "It was a long time ago."

"Oh. Well, let's keep looking, I guess."

For fifteen minutes, Carmen searched, her sandwich forgotten. She uncovered only the same websites we had, leading nowhere. The cashier came by to tell her that her break was almost over, but she shooed him away, her gaze fixed on the screen. With her lips parted and her laptop's blue glow glazing her glasses lenses, Carmen looked like how Naomi got when watching *SpongeBob*.

At last, she sighed and leaned back in her chair, taking off her glasses to rub the bridge of her nose. "I'm sorry, but I can't find anything. If there's something about that symbol online, it's not on Google."

As she began to lower the lid of her laptop, Sandra leaned forward in her seat. "Wait. Ash, what did you say that name was again?"

"Alcántara," he said.

"Carmen, look that up."

"Okay," she said, and brought up the Google tab again.

Her new search delivered a few images of rolling brown fields, a tall bridge decorated with archways, and a river so blue it looked as though it had been dyed. Ancient stone buildings rose from the hillside, crested by a church's spire.

"This is in Spain," I said, reading the first two links. "Ash, do you remember when you were here?"

He shook his head, his face growing paler by the moment, "No, but I remember the smoke. And the screams."

I shivered, haunted by the look in his eyes. No moisture ran down his face, but it almost seemed like he was on the verge of crying.

"Maybe there's something on the Spanish Google page," Carmen said, opening it in a new window. The websites that came up with her search might as well have been gibberish to me, but she and Sandra leaned forward, reading under their breaths.

"Click that one," Sandra said, pointing to the fifth link down the page.

The website was decorated with a banner that looked like it had been taken from a medieval document—sweeping lines of sepia-brown ink highlighted with faded dabs of yellow, blue, and red. In the illustration, a cluster of people huddled together, flames licking at their feet. I thought it was a scene of hell, but it took me a moment to recognize that instead of being tormented by pitchfork-wielding demons, the group stood atop a burning pyre. Their faces were so serene, as though they had already accepted what was happening to them. As though they deserved it completely.

"What is this?" I whispered, looking over at Sandra.

"The Spanish Inquisition," she said grimly, her brown eyes darkening.

My mouth puckered like I'd stepped in dog poop. We had learned about the Spanish Inquisition for a few class periods last year, when our history unit had touched upon the subject of medieval Europe. Our teacher had taught us that the Inquisition had burned witches and heretics, but when I had asked my mom for help with the homework assignment, she had revealed to me that the truth was far darker. Those "heretics" had largely been Jews and Muslims who had converted to Christianity in order to avoid being expelled from Spanish territory, along with smaller numbers of Christians.

Carmen scrolled down the page, revealing another image from a medieval manuscript—a line of individuals in red robes, carrying banners adorned with the same image that had been engraved on the gold pendant. Then, in the second page, she came across a painting that took my breath away. It was a ring engraved with the seal of Solomon.

17

"'KNIGHTS OF THE APOCALYPSE,'" Sandra read under her breath, translating the Spanish for my benefit. "It says here that they're an ancient order dating back to the Inquisition."

She was about to say more when the cashier popped his head in. Scratching at the mole on his chin, he hollered, "Carmen, you really ought to get back to work or Mr. Duncan's going to be peeved."

Carmen sighed, running a hand through her bright blue hair. Snagging the bag of chips, she rose to her feet. "You guys can keep using my laptop. Just bring it out when you're done. And help yourselves to the rest of my sandwich. Don't be shy. I see you eyeing it, Ash."

With a chuckle, she stepped out of the room. Ash groaned and pushed the sandwich back across the table, scooting his chair away like the tuna had been dumped in a barrel of radioactive waste.

He eyed the sandwich. "You humans are truly repulsive. I don't understand how you can enjoy fish and cheese."

"Weren't you the one who ate four slices of anchovy pizza?"

Ash scowled. "This is different."

"You sure? Why don't you give it a try?"

"I'd sooner swallow my own tongue," he said with a glare, clearly unamused.

"Why don't you like fish anyway?" I asked.

"They remind me of God," he said flatly.

Yeah, that sounded like something a demon would say.

Rolling my eyes, I turned back to Sandra. "What else does the website say?"

"Oh, this is dark." She nibbled her lower lip. "So, apparently, as the Inquisitors were hunting down people, the Knights of the Apocalypse were searching for biblical relics. Not just the Ring of Solomon, but also the Ark of the Covenant, the Staff of Moses, Holy Grail, and others."

I threw up my hands. "Great. So, they're basically the *Indiana Jones* Nazis."

"That and worse. It says here that at first, they were searching for those artifacts at the behest of the king, but over time their mission changed. They became fixated on finding the Ring of Solomon, which it says here is capable of controlling demons."

Sandra and I gave Ash the side-eye.

"What?" he asked, seeming baffled.

"Is there anything else you'd like to tell us this ring is capable of?" I asked. "I mean, aside from the whole 'talking to animals, controlling demons' thing?"

"Well…"

"It's not just demons the ring is able to awaken," Sandra said grimly. "The Knights of the Apocalypse believed that by awakening the three beasts created at the dawn of the world—the Behemoth, the Leviathan, and the Ziz—they will summon someone called Armilus. This website says Armilus is, I quote, 'a false messiah equivalent to the dajjal in Islam and the antichrist in Christianity.'"

"Antichrist? You mean like in *The Omen*?" I gave it more thought. "You know, Sandra, I've got a feeling this Armilus person is already walking the earth—he's in our homeroom, and his name is Jeffrey."

Rolling her eyes, Sandra pushed me gently in the shoulder before turning her attention back to the screen. "The Knights' leader and his followers were excommunicated and charged with witchcraft and demon worship in the late 1500s, and after that the surviving Knights left Spain. But I guess they never gave up on their search."

"Great, so they're demon worshippers now too!" I said sarcastically. "As if this can't get any worse."

"It doesn't say here what they hope will happen once they do summon Armilus." Sandra turned. "Ash, do you know?"

"The end of days," Ash said quietly. "The ruin of all things."

"Who'd even want that?" I asked, appalled.

"There are some who believe that paradise will rise from the ruin. But some day, you will learn that there are also people in this world who simply take delight in the suffering of others. Which breed of human our ring thief is, I can't say."

"Considering he threw me into a lion pit, I'd say there's a ninety percent chance it's the second one." I groaned. "I'm not even Christian, and I'm horrible at being Jewish. I didn't ask to get wrapped up in this. First the literal king of demons, and now three gigantic beasts, and the antichrist. You've got to be kidding me."

"Well, excuse me. I didn't ask for this either," Sandra snapped. "Maybe you should have just left that strange ring alone instead of buying it."

"My bad. How could I know that something so gaudy looking would end up being so powerful?"

"Stop arguing, you two," Ash said, acting like a grown-up for once. "There's an easy solution to all this."

Sandra eyed him a bit warily. "And what would that be?"

"Simple. All we have to do is wait for the first beast to be summoned and then stop it. All three creatures must walk the earth at the same time, so by defeating the Leviathan or the Behemoth, that will put quite a damper on the Knights' plans. Or at least long enough for us to get the ring back."

"How are we supposed to stop a giant monster?" I asked, my face heating up in anger. Ash was the reason for all this, and he wasn't even acting worried.

He shrugged. "If you hit a demon enough times, it'll go back to sleep beneath the earth. Even one as great as myself."

"Can't you just shoot a laser beam at it or something?" I asked. "You're the king of demons. Don't you have anything useful you can do?"

His eyes narrowed. "Excuse me?"

"I'm just saying, for the king of demons, so far you've been pretty lame."

"Zach, shut up," Sandra said quickly, her face blanching.

"I mean, seriously," I blabbed, feeling like my mouth had decided to run off on its own. "Woo-hoo, I'm Ashmedai, the king of demons. What can I do? Oh, yeah, I can nearly impale us on a tree branch, and I got us into this whole stupid mess. Aside from that, I'm utterly useless!"

"Hold your tongue, human," Ash said curtly. "Remember to whom you are talking."

"Oh, I know full well. A pip-squeak of a demon king who ended up ruining our entire lives."

Ever since he had come into my life, everything had exploded. I should have known this was what happened when you summoned a demon. It wasn't all just fun and games.

"You know what? I wish I never summoned you in the first place. I should've just left you inside the ring!" Before I knew what I was doing, I picked up Carmen's leftover tuna fish sandwich and hurled it at him. It landed on his chest, spurting gooey cheese, chunks of tuna, and the atrociously orange special sauce across his T-shirt.

"So be it then." Ash stepped forward, his eyes glowing. He crushed the fallen sandwich bun beneath his shoes, while the remnants of the sandwich still encrusted to his shirt began to smolder and flake away as soot. "I hope you enjoy your last few days on earth. I know I'll be enjoying mine."

He strode from the room, vanishing the moment he stepped into the hall. Through the open door, I watched as comics spewed to the floor as though knocked down by an invisible hand. The front door swung open on its own and slammed shut with such force, cracks spiderwebbed across the glass pane.

As Carmen and the cashier stared in shock at the wreckage, Sandra turned to me. The blood had drained from her face. "What did you just do?"

"I—"

"You just threw a tuna fish sandwich at our only chance at saving the world. You realize that?"

I searched for a response. "I'm sorry. I don't know what came over me. It's like my mind just walked off on its own."

"So, what are we supposed to do now?" she asked.

"Buy a lot of sunscreen to protect us from the hellfire?" I offered weakly.

She shook her head in disgust and rose to her feet.

"Where are you going?" I called after her as she walked from the room.

"Somewhere far away from you," she said. "Just in case stupidity is catching."

I groaned. This wasn't the worst argument Sandra and I had gotten into, but it came pretty close to that. On top of the added bonus of accidentally causing the apocalypse, this was probably the worst day of my life.

And by the sound of it, I didn't have many days left.

18

"HAPPY BIRTHDAY TO YOU," Naomi sang off-key, tottering forward with a glass tray holding our mom's birthday cake. "Happy birthday to you."

"Careful, Naomi," I said as the chocolate cake swayed precariously. Luckily, the candles on it weren't lit, or she might end up burning the whole house down.

She set it on the table, avoiding yet another disaster to add to this miserable day. After returning home from the comics store, I had spent the rest of the evening moping around and watching funny cat videos in bed. I'd expected Ash to appear at any moment or at least raid the fridge, but if he was still nearby, he hadn't revealed himself to me.

Now, it took all my self-control just to sit through Naomi's shrill, off-key rendition of the "Happy Birthday" song, grumbling along sullenly while she and my dad sang it to my mom. I caught my mom's eye from across the table, and she offered me an amused little smile and a soft roll of her eyes, as if to say, *Let's get this over with.*

I felt closer to my mom than to my dad, but I didn't feel ready to come out to her yet. Or either of them, for that matter. They weren't religious, so it wasn't like they were going to call an exorcist to pray the gay away, but still. Every time I even considered telling them, my throat closed up and I couldn't get a word out. Deep down, there was still the fear that once I told them, once I really owned it, nothing would ever be the same.

"Sounds like you had a big day, Zach," Dad said and raised his eyebrows. "From what I heard, there was a bit of excitement at the zoo."

"Yeah, it sounds like some kid fell into the lion pit," I said with a nervous laugh. "Stupid, right? I didn't see it, but I guess he got out okay."

"I wish I could've gone to the zoo," Naomi piped up, pouting.

"We'll go for your birthday," Dad told her, ruffling her flossy blond hair. "As long as you promise not to fall into any enclosures."

Mom shook her head in dismay. "You'd think the management there would take better precautions."

"They're probably more worried about the animals escaping than people trying to get in," I said, clearing my throat. Time to change the subject before my parents started grilling me. "Anyway, happy birthday, Mom. Naomi and I bought you something."

As I pulled out the small box I had hidden in the pocket of my hoodie, Naomi stared at me slack-jawed from across the table.

She was probably imagining the tyranny our mom would carry out with the entire animal kingdom at her mercy. If I'd been in a better mood, I would've really drawn out the suspense.

"Oh, you two shouldn't have," Mom said, taking the box from me. She tugged the ribbon free and lifted the lid. "Oh, it's beautiful."

It wasn't Jewish, but it was very gaudy—a butterfly encrusted with sparkling rhinestones that I bought from a thrift store on the bike ride home with my surviving ten dollars. As Mom pinned it to her shirt, Dad lit the candles on the cake.

We sang "Happy Birthday" a second time, but I couldn't put my heart in it. If I didn't get the ring back, this might be one of the last birthdays we celebrated. Talk about depressing.

"Make a wish," Dad said, and my mom blew out the candles.

"What'd you wish for?" Naomi pestered, leaning over the table.

"It won't come true if you tell," Mom said with a wink.

My throat tightened. Even if she'd kept the wish to herself, there wasn't enough time now anyway for it to come true. There wasn't enough time for anything. Soon, the three beasts would be awakened, and who knew what might happen then?

"I think you're old enough to get a man-sized piece," my dad joked, setting a heaping slice on my plate. The frosting was cloyingly sweet and settled in my stomach like the baker had swapped it out for cement. After a few bites, I lowered my fork.

"What's the matter?" Mom asked. "You love chocolate."

"I ate a big lunch," I muttered, putting my fork down. "I'll just save the rest for tomorrow."

"What's gotten into him?" my dad asked on my way out the door.

"Puberty," my mom said with a shiver of dread, like puberty was accompanied by an inevitable werewolf transformation.

Naomi caught up with me at my bedroom door. "Zach, where's the ring? Come on, you can't keep it all for yourself. That's not fair."

"I'm not."

She puffed out her lower lip. "Then let me see it!"

I ushered her into my room. As I shut the door behind us, I took a deep breath, preparing myself. "I lost it, Naomi."

"Lost it?!" she shrieked.

"Not so loud," I hissed. "Look, the ring was bad business anyway. Just let it go."

Her fingers traced my cheek and came back glistening with clear droplets. "Zach, why are you crying?"

I twisted away, gritting my teeth to hold back the sobs that came dangerously close to escaping my throat. I sat at the side of my bed and shook my head. "I'm sorry. I love you, Naomi. I'm so sorry."

19

"ZACH!" MY MOM called downstairs. "You have a visitor."

Groaning, I cracked open my eyes and wiped my mouth with the back of my hand. Crawling out of bed like a raccoon from a trash can, I hitched up my pajama pants and stumbled downstairs. Deep afternoon sunlight slanted through the windows. It was later than I expected.

Mom and Dad allowed me and Naomi one cheat day each quarter, where we could stay home from school, as long as we told them the reason why. They said it was better than having us lie to them or play sick, and even kids needed a break every now and then. Most of the time, Naomi and I didn't use our cheat days because of the free-pan-pizza coupon you got for perfect attendance. Except, this morning I'd figured that the whole "beasts of the apocalypse" thing might put even Domino's out of business.

When I told my mom I wanted to stay home, something in

my face must've startled her, because she hadn't questioned me one bit. I'd spent the entire day trying to read all the books my parents had bought for me but that I'd never gotten around to actually reading. Instead, all I could think about was Ash and the end of the world, and eventually I had just gone to sleep so I wouldn't have to agonize over it anymore.

As I reached the bottom of the stairs, Sandra barreled through the front door. She probably rode her bike here, because her dark bob was molded in the shape of a helmet. At the sight of me, she gave a disapproving snort. "Seriously? You ditched school today just so you could sleep in?"

"Excuse me if I want to spend my last days on earth doing my favorite thing," I said dryly, rubbing the back of my head.

"No way. That's not how this is going to work." She followed me up to my room and unzipped her backpack, pulling out a water bottle. "Here."

"Thanks." I cracked open the lid and took a gulp, glad to wash away the nasty taste of sleep from my mouth.

"No, don't drink it all!" she said in horror. "That's holy water."

"Seriously? It tastes like tap water." Tentatively, I took another sip. "It's not even that good. Are you sure it's holy water?"

"Well, yeah. I stole it from the font at church on my way to school."

I sprayed out the second mouthful. "What?"

"There's a little font in front, for you to dip your hand in and make the sign of the cross." She mimicked the gesture for me. "'Por la señal de la Santa Cruz, de nuestros enemigos. Libranos, Señor, Dios Nuestro,' as my mom says."

I stared at the half-empty bottle. "So, you're telling me I just drank something that a gazillion people washed their hands in?"

"Well, excuse me." She rolled her eyes. "Holy water isn't easy to come by. It doesn't exactly grow on trees, Zach."

I twisted the cap back on and tossed her the bottle. "What are we supposed to do with this? Ash is already gone, and the ring is too. We can't exorcise him."

"That's for the monsters."

"I don't think a water bottle filled with holy water is going to kill them." I'd seen enough movies to know that you had to get creative when it came to taking down demons. As in, "tuna fish and chain saw" creative.

"Of course not. So, let's get down to business." She reached into her bag, pulling out a cardboard box of firecrackers and a Swiss Army knife. "This was all I could come up with. What do you have?"

"Uh…" Trailing off, I looked around my room. I didn't exactly think we'd have much luck pelting biblical monsters with action figures or comic books. "Nothing?"

"Oh, come on." She groaned. "Doesn't your mom have something in her collection?"

I gave it some thought. "You know, that's actually not a bad idea. But first, let me get out of my pajamas. This is way too early for this."

"It's almost four," she said in exasperation, but sat on my bed as I got ready.

I didn't like how I looked in the bathroom mirror. Even after taking a nap, sleepless circles darkened my eyelids, while yanking a brush through my hair only managed to make it even messier. After a few attempts at combing the wild frizz into submission, I gave up. A bad-hair day was the least of my worries.

"Where do you think Ash is?" Sandra asked as I joined her in the bedroom.

"Who cares? We don't need him."

We went down to the kitchen and rummaged through the china cabinet containing my mom's Judaica collection. I didn't think there was much power in the kitschy ceramic figurines of klezmer players, and none of the menorahs were heavy enough to knock a monster clean out, but there had to be something in there that could help us. Shoving aside a bunch of old books in one of the bottom cabinets, I glimpsed the hard sheen of metal.

I picked up the knife and turned it around in my hands. The serrated edge was sharp enough that I was afraid to test my thumb against it, and the blade alone was longer than my forearm.

"What does this mean?" Sandra asked, tracing her finger down the row of letters engraved on the flat edge of the blade.

שדק תבש

I blushed, racking my brain for an answer. It might as well have been Sanskrit. I had only gone to a few Hebrew lessons before Naomi's soccer practice, and my boredom, and my parents' own busy work schedule, and not enough cash had permanently benched any chance of having a bar mitzvah ceremony once I turned thirteen. Not that I really cared. Until now,

I hadn't thought I'd ever actually need to read Hebrew—it had never felt like a part of my own history, not when my mom's ancestors had come from Belarus and my dad could practically trace his roots back to the *Mayflower*.

"I don't know," I said lamely when I realized Sandra was still waiting for a response.

Sandra blinked. "How don't you know?"

I sighed. She knew Spanish thanks to her parents, but the last time anyone in my family tree had spoken Hebrew was probably back in the Stone Age, or at least Belarus.

"Nobody bothered to teach me," I said. "Even my mom can't speak it."

"Do you think it's a prayer?" she asked.

"Yeah, let's go with that," I said, even though I was pretty sure that the only thing my mom had used this knife for was to cut bread. I tucked it in my backpack just as my mom came into the kitchen.

She blinked in surprise, adjusting her reading glasses. "What are you two doing over there?"

"I was just showing Sandra your collection," I said, closing the cabinet drawer.

Mom turned to Sandra. "Did something catch your eye?"

"Uh, yeah." Sandra looked at the shelves before pointing at the tiny golem figurine perched on a stack of faded tintypes.

"Ah, this is one of my favorites." As my mom picked up the figurine, a familiar gleam entered her eyes. I groaned inwardly, steeling myself for a history lesson. "It's modern, but I couldn't resist. It's modeled after the famous Golem of Prague, a creature shaped from clay and brought to life in order to protect the Czech Jewish community. Of course, like all legends, it doesn't end well, and the creature eventually turns on its creator and has to be destroyed."

As Mom returned the figurine to its shelf, I zipped up my backpack, glad she hadn't noticed the knife's absence yet. No way would I be able to explain *that*.

"There's one other thing I was curious about," Sandra said, and I shot her a pleading look. If she kept Mom going, we'd be stuck here all day.

Mom smiled. "Of course."

"Zach was telling me about the three beasts that were created at the beginning of time. You know, the Behemoth, the Leviathan, and uh—"

"The Ziz," my mom said.

"Yeah. So, like, he was saying they're supposed to bring the apocalypse, and we're doing an RPG—you know, like D&D—where we're going to bring them into the story. I'm the Dungeon master, so I need to know, how would you know when one of the monsters was coming? I mean, would fire rain from the sky or something?"

Mom chuckled. "I'll admit, I'm not an expert on this part of the folklore. But I imagine, if these beasts do exist, and they do in fact bring the end times, then the sign of their awakening would be cataclysmic."

20

"CATACLYSMIC," I SAID as we pedaled our bikes down the street. "That doesn't sound ominous at all."

"There it is again." Sandra glanced back at me with a smile. "The negativity."

"Says the girl who dresses like Wednesday Addams." I sighed, falling into place beside her. Overhead, the sun winked down from the bright blue sky. There was nothing to suggest the apocalypse was upon us—no ominous choir music, no doomsday preachers ranting at the street corners, not even a rain cloud. "So, what now?"

"We find Ash."

I didn't want to rely on him, but she was right. We could use a bit of divine intervention, even if it was the sort to come from a demon. He'd helped build the First Temple after all. Compared to that, putting down a monster would be a piece of cake.

"He couldn't have gone far," Sandra said. "He's probably just hanging around, waiting for the first beast to appear."

"More like eating his way through America. I'll bet you five dollars we're going to find him at a pizza parlor or ice-cream shop."

"But not a fish-and-chips place," Sandra said with a laugh.

I grinned, unable to help myself. "Did you see his face when Carmen pulled out that tuna melt?"

"I don't blame him. It smelled awful." She hesitated, and her smile faded by a degree, turning almost sheepish. "So, about Carmen… I maaaay have told her about the whole demon-king thing."

I sputtered for a response. "What? Why?"

"Hey, don't look at me like that. What was I supposed to tell her? I mean, Ash just disappeared, and he basically wrecked half the store in the process."

I sighed. She had a point. "How did your cousin take it?"

"Surprisingly, not as bad as I expected. I mean, I'm not sure if she believes it, but there wasn't really any other way to explain what happened yesterday."

I felt strangely relieved. There was one less thing we had to worry about, and it was nice knowing we had a teenager on our side.

As I was about to say more, I heard the sudden rattling of gravel, like a car was approaching. I glanced around, nervous that the man from the zoo had come back to finish what the lions had failed to accomplish.

The street was deserted. Then, slowly, it dawned on me— the noise was coming from all directions.

I braked to a stop and looked down. The pebbles jittered on the blacktop. At first, the rumbling was so subtle that I barely even felt it, but in the matter of moments, it grew beneath my feet until the whole earth seemed to quake. We staggered off our bikes as the nearby homes trembled and the trees swayed and snapped.

Sandra spread her arms to stabilize herself. "An earthquake?!"

Just when I thought the ground would open beneath us, everything went still. Dead still. But in the trembling's place, I could still feel a disturbance hanging in the air, like a satellite had gone out of orbit and was plummeting straight toward us, falling faster by the moment.

"No way," I whispered.

Sandra gulped, looking around. "Is the monster here?"

The hairs rose on the nape of my neck, and a tingling swept down my spine. There was a feeling in the air, not just of something falling, but of electricity, like the static before a storm.

Gravel scraped across the asphalt. I watched as the tiny pebbles and sand particles rolled past my sneakers as though drawn by a magnetic pull toward a strange and alien source. Even as the pebbles went still, I sensed the force's pull, guiding south toward the low hills at San Pancras's outskirts. Could it be the old cement factory?

"Follow me," I said, swinging my leg over my bike. As we pedaled down the street, a flock of crows broke from the trees ahead, swooping and cawing. Within moments, they were joined by numerous sparrows, hawks, and falcons, prey and predator alike flooding the sky in a dark exodus.

Fleeing.

21

BIRDS BLACKENED THE SKY, sending loose feathers cascading down. As we reached the neighborhood we'd passed through the day before, Sandra twisted her bike in a sharp turn, narrowly avoiding being plowed into by a minivan as she headed in the direction of the comic shop.

"Come on!" she shouted, glancing back at me. "Carmen has a license. She can give us a ride."

"Are you sure we should involve her?" I shouted back. "I mean, more than we already have?"

Sandra grinned. "Trust me, she loves those supernatural shows. Saving the world, fighting monsters, teaming up with the king of demons. It'll be more than she could hope for. The last time she would've had this much fun was when she went to Comic Con."

Carmen was lounging at the register when we entered the store, resting her chin on her knuckles as she swiped boredly through her phone. She glanced up as the bell rang above the door and sat up quickly, her eyes bright with excitement.

"What are you two doing here? Did you feel that trembling a little while ago?"

"We're pretty sure it's one of the monsters," Sandra said, earning a befuddled look from two teens who were browsing the shelves. "It came in the direction of the abandoned factory."

"I knew it felt close!" Carmen said, lurching to her feet. As she stepped from behind the counter, she twisted her head toward the other end of the store. "Hey, Michael, take over my shift, will you?"

"Really?" the boy shouted from deeper in, out of sight. "In case you didn't notice, I'm busy cleaning up the mess on the floor. Come on, I'm buried up to my knees in comic books here."

"I'll owe you one. I'll bring you a free tuna melt next time I go to the sub place."

I groaned inwardly.

From the other end of the store, there came no response. Her coworker was probably estimating the chances of dying from indigestion. At last, the boy shouted back, "Buy me an Italian sub, and it's a deal."

"Deal." Grinning, she turned to us and pushed her glasses up the bridge of her nose. "What are you two waiting for? Just leave your bikes here with Michael. We're driving in style!"

Driving "in style" turned out to mean crammed in the back seat of Carmen's ancient Buick as tightly as canned sardines. Like an impatient kid waiting in line for a roller-coaster ride,

Carmen bumped up and down in her seat as she gripped the steering wheel. "Which monster do you two think it is?"

"I'm not sure," I said. I hadn't bothered to do my research since leaving the comic bookstore the day before. I had been too busy sulking to think about fighting the three beasts of legend head-on.

As the car roared out of the parking lot, I gripped on to the edge of my seat. Carmen twisted the steering wheel, sending us in a violent swerve across two lanes of traffic before the car steadied. If the monster didn't kill us, I was pretty sure her driving would finish the job.

"We did a little more research after you left," Sandra told me, looking blissfully oblivious to Carmen's horrible driving, even as her chin-length black hair was jostled into an unkempt nest. After a particularly fierce jolt, she lifted her hands and smoothed her hair back into a bob. "The Leviathan is a water monster, while the Ziz is supposed to be a giant bird, and the Behemoth is some sort of land creature. So, if it's awakened on dry ground, I'll bet it's the Behemoth."

"Maybe we should call in the army," I said, even though I doubted that they would consider it anything more than a prank call. "I mean, they handled Godzilla in the movies, right?"

"I don't think we have time for that," Carmen said, stomping down on the gas pedal. The car jolted forward so quickly that its tires squealed against the pavement and my stomach flip-flopped. For a terrifying moment, I was afraid she was about to lose control of the car and grabbed hold of the dangly oh-crap handle above the door. After a nauseating shudder, the car steadied, and we rolled forward smoothly, turning onto the side road that led into the mountains.

"Your cousin is a horrible driver," I whispered to Sandra.

She rolled her eyes. "She hasn't gotten into an accident yet at least."

Several hundred yards down the side road, the asphalt became gravel, and then rain-washed dirt, eroded from years of rainfall, and studded with roots and exposed rocks. Carmen was forced to continue at a slower pace, the car trundling along like a pack mule on its last legs.

My parents and I hiked here every now and then, if we didn't feel like tackling the hills and ravines of the nearby Rancho Corral de Tierra. The land was less steep but still hilly and untamed. We weren't allowed to go near the abandoned cement factory, but from the tops of hills, it was visible against the brush—tall gray towers and a sprawl of graffiti-tagged buildings.

As we headed deeper into the wilderness, movement flickered between the clumps of bushes and trees—blurs of gray and brown only visible for a moment through the greenery, before disappearing once more. It took me a moment to recognize those flashes of movement as fleeing coyotes and gray foxes. Among the animals, I also spotted a mountain lion and what I was pretty sure was either a man in a costume or Mothman itself. Before I could point out the possible cryptid sighting to Carmen, the ground ahead split apart with a deafening roar.

Carmen slammed on the brakes, bringing us to a screeching halt. The crack widened, engulfing the roadside and sending dirt pouring into its bottomless crevice.

"No way!" Carmen yanked the gearshift to Reverse. We screeched back three feet before another crack split the road behind us, cutting off our escape route.

"Not good, not good," she whispered frantically, her eyes widening behind her clunky black glasses.

"Everyone, out of the car now," Sandra shouted.

We scrambled out of the Buick, throwing ourselves onto solid ground as the earth shook furiously. The car slipped into the abyss, and Carmen howled in horror. "Not my baby!"

My attention was on something else. Staring at the pit that had cut off our route, I watched in shock and horror as an enormous paw emerged from the crevice.

22

SIX FINGERS CURLED around the edge of the ravine, tipped with hooked black claws. Coarse brown fur covered the back of the hand, which looked almost humanlike, except for the extra finger.

"What is that thing?" My voice cracked, only this time out of fear instead of the accursed effects of puberty.

"The Behemoth," Sandra said gravely.

The creature wiggled free of the crevice. Crouching on all fours, it stood nearly as tall as an elephant and was twice as long. Fur covered its apelike body, cloaking the muscular folds of its stomach and arms. Its face was long and horselike, and tusks curled from the sides of its mouth, ending in lethal points. As its yellow eyes landed on us, its dark lips peeled back to reveal a nest of jagged fangs.

"Sandra, the holy water!" I shouted, reeling back from the monster.

While I had been too busy gawking at King Kong here, she had already retrieved the plastic bottle from her backpack and twisted off the cap. She threw the bottle at the Behemoth, and the container struck it head-on, drenching its face in holy water.

"Yes!" She pumped her fist.

Droplets raced down the Behemoth's long muzzle. It licked the water off, apparently thirsty after a long sleep underground. And if the creature was anything like Ash, it'd be hungry too.

Great. Forget about the rest of the pathetic stockpile Sandra and I had put together. I doubted even the army's weapons would be able to take this thing down. Time to improvise.

"Run!" I shouted, pivoting on my heel as the Behemoth charged at us. We fled across the rolling hillside.

Keeping pace with me, Sandra pointed ahead. "Over there!"

In the distance, the cement factory's buildings glinted through the trees like a dinosaur's sun-bleached bones. When we had come here in the past, my parents had warned me about the dangers of going off the trail and how the entire area was riddled with old machinery. Maybe there was something in the ruins that could help us.

We raced for the cover of the old factory. Behind us, the Behemoth roared. Afraid to look behind me, I ran even faster, my lungs screaming in my chest. If I survived this, I was never gonna complain about PE again!

Blind with terror, I fled into the ruins' shadows, scrambling over piles of rubble and twisted metal poles. The ground was a minefield of nails and broken glass, the stuff of mothers' nightmares, and I knew that if I fell, my hands would be cut to pieces.

Behind me, I heard Carmen's and Sandra's own frantic gasps, and then the panting of the Behemoth. It was getting closer.

At the far end of the compound was the factory itself, a decaying cement building with tall smokestacks rising from the roof. I prayed the double doors at the front wouldn't be barricaded like the boarded-over windows.

As we reached it, I tested the handle. It practically came off in my hand, the lock already bashed in by some overenthusiastic vandal. I threw open the doors and barreled inside, Sandra and Carmen close behind me.

When I glanced over my shoulder me as I ran, my breath caught in my throat. The beast had managed to squeeze through the broken door. Bits of rubble crumbled from the walls as it entered, and the surviving hinges snapped free and clanged to the floor.

Grayish beams of light reached through the cracks in the boarded-over windows, illuminating the hallway ahead. The walls were darkened in the patina of black mold and graffiti, and the plaster looked slick in places, as if we had fled into the gullet of a creature even larger than the one hunting us relentlessly.

I twisted down one hall then another, retreating deeper into the labyrinth of dark, grimy passages. Doorways opened into abandoned rooms, some nearly filled to the brim with junk, others empty except for a single eerie relic, like a bucket or an orange corduroy sofa. Too late, I realized that Sandra and Carmen were no longer at my side. From close behind me came the snap of tiles beneath the Behemoth's colossal body.

As I risked another look back, a thin groan of terror escaped my lips. The monster was twenty feet away and gaining, its yellow eyes radiating an eerie light, like they were filled with glow-stick fluid. It loped forward on all fours, muscles bulging beneath its short pelt.

As I caught a glimpse of the Behemoth's fangs dripping with long strings of drool, I spewed enough swear words to land me a month-long grounding. Why did I have to throw that tuna fish sandwich at Ash? He was probably gorging his way through San Pancras's restaurant district right now, leaving numerous waitstaff with magic-induced brain damage thanks to being cashless. Meanwhile, I was about to become a demon's dinner!

Reaching a corner, I pivoted on my heel and took a right turn down the next hallway. Behind me, the Behemoth's claws skidded across the floor.

Ahead, the windows were boarded over completely, and shadows reigned. A strange, bulky shape filled the hallway. Too late, I realized it was a pile of crates and ladders. I twisted around to go the other way, but the Behemoth was already lumbering down the hall, its fur coated in white plaster dust.

Turning back ahead, I took a deep breath and darted toward the blockade. I squeezed between the stacks of crates and clambered over others, nearly getting squashed when a ladder came crashing down behind me with a deafening clang. Somehow, I made it out whole, with all my limbs intact, and scrambled across the floor as the Behemoth barreled through the heap of junk.

The clatter and screech of twisting metal echoed through the hall. I glanced back, my breath escaping in a relieved sigh. The Behemoth sprawled on the floor, its limbs entangled in the rubble. Hissing at me, it bared its teeth. A forked tongue flicked out between its fangs.

"Yeah, that's what you get!" I shouted triumphantly.

One of the ladders snapped right in two as the Behemoth thrashed against it, snarling now. Oh crap. I kept running, not waiting to see how long the entrapment would hold. Okay, horror movie tip #1: don't taunt monsters, even when they're down.

I tried to loop back to the entrance, but I couldn't find my way out. Charging through a pair of double doors, I entered an enormous room at the heart of the facility. Strange machines loomed in the darkness like silent beasts, teethed with rusty cogs.

I ducked behind a tall cylindrical vat, pressing my palm over my mouth to muffle my ragged gasps. Heart pounding a mile a minute, I crouched there, listening to the Behemoth's claws scratch against the walls deeper into the factory.

It was hunting.

Just as I began to lower my fingers from over my mouth, a hand fell on my shoulder. I yelped, swiveling around.

"Be quiet," Sandra hissed, squatting down beside me. In her black-and-gray plaid skirt and black shirt, she blended into the shadows. Meanwhile, I was the idiot who'd thrown on a green

T-shirt dyed so brightly that the Behemoth would probably think I was lime flavored.

I cleared my throat, a bit embarrassed by the squeak I'd made, but at least I hadn't pissed myself—or worse, done a number two. "Where's Carmen?"

"We got separated." She swallowed hard. "I think she's still out there."

"She'll be okay." I placed my hand on her shoulder, trying to muster up some cheerfulness even though I was pretty sure Carmen was Behemoth chow by now. "She's a highschooler, so she can handle herself."

"What should we do?" Sandra asked as I peeked out from behind the tank. Still no sign of the Behemoth, but I could hear its claws scraping across the floor. The groan of splintering wood echoed from deeper in, followed by the creature's growl.

"Do you still have your backpack?" I asked.

She lifted it in one hand.

"If holy water couldn't hurt it, we're going to need something with more boom."

"The firecrackers," she whispered, and I nodded.

While she dug around in her pack, I picked up my mom's knife, which Sandra had placed on the floor. It didn't even look sharp enough to give the Behemoth a haircut, much less draw blood.

"Aha," Sandra said, her eyes brightening. "Found them."

As she drew the cardboard box from her backpack, the door flung open. Carmen rushed inside and braced the double doors with her spread arms, before her eyes landed on us.

"Help me block this door," she shouted, her gaze roving around desperately. "Over there, that pole. Bring it over. Quickly!"

Sandra and I rushed out from behind cover. I snatched up the metal pole she was talking about, a narrow but heavy rebar like the kind used to reinforce cement. Carmen stuck the pole through the door handles as if this were a castle under siege, and just in time too—moments later, the double doors shuddered in violent impact.

From the other side, the Behemoth roared. I grimaced at the shrill squeal of its claws scraping down the metal panels.

"I don't think that door's going to hold for long," I said as we backed away. There was nowhere left to run—the bay doors at the other end of the room were padlocked, and the only window was the multipaned glass ceiling forty feet above.

"We need a plan," Carmen said, pushing her glasses up her nose from where they had fallen askew.

"We were going to throw fireworks at it," Sandra said, and her cousin groaned.

"Seriously, prima? Who'd you steal those from? Your brother?"

Sandra gulped. "Maybe."

"You'll blow your fingers off with those." Carmen eyed the knife I held awkwardly at my side. "And something tells me if you start waving that bread knife around, you won't end up much better, Zach."

"Excuse me, but you're not exactly coming up with a better idea," I snapped back, then grimaced as the door shuddered once more. The hinges squealed, straining under the force of the Behemoth's charging body.

154

"Let me think." Carmen's gaze swept over the rusty junk heaped across the factory floor. Crossing the room, she leaned down and picked up a coiled metal cord from the ground. Made of woven wire, the cable disappeared at the other end through a hole drilled in the floor. She gave it one tug, then another, and it held steadily. Smiling, Carmen turned to us. "I have a plan."

23

CROUCHED BEHIND THE BARRELS, I flinched as the door shuddered once more, the hinges squealing in protest. Each time the Behemoth crashed against the steel panel, the bar Carmen had thrust between the door handles trembled and shifted. Less than an inch more and the rod would fall.

Across the room, I caught a glimpse of Sandra and Carmen hiding behind a stack of barrels. Our eyes met. Carmen gave a thumbs-up, but I didn't feel optimistic enough to return it. Teen or not, I was beginning to wonder if we should trust the instincts of someone who ate the most atrocious tuna melts in the world.

I flinched as the door came crashing down with a thunderous bang, gritting my teeth to keep from crying out. The Behemoth prowled into the room on all fours, knuckles dragging. Its nostrils flared as it sniffed at the air.

My breath seized up. Could it smell us?

Stepping into the center of the room, the beast paused in the bar of sunlight that filtered through the glass ceiling. The light gleamed across a knobbed rod of golden metal embedded in its right shoulder. My eyes narrowed. What was that? Could it be something like the ring, or even Ash's cuff?

I was torn from my thoughts by the creature's panting. Its lantern-bright eyes flickered over my hiding place before scanning the rest of the room. I gulped. Where was the king of demons when we needed him?

Swallowing down the lump that built in my throat, I edged out from behind the barrel. This better work; otherwise, my next appearance on this mortal plane might be in the form of demon dung.

The Zippo lighter Sandra had stolen from her brother was running on fumes. It took several flicks of the wheel to make a pathetic little flame. Holding my breath, I held the flame to the firecracker's fuse, remembering my mom's warnings about lost fingers and burned skin. She had a meltdown the one time I played with a Fourth of July sparkler, and if she saw what I was doing now, she'd go nuclear.

The moment the fuse began to burn, I hurled the firecracker to the opposite end of the room. The Behemoth twisted in that direction, strings of drool flying from its mouth.

The firecracker exploded into a fizzle of blue sparks. With a roar, the Behemoth lumbered toward the glow, so distracted by the light show that it didn't notice the metal cable stretched across the floor at ankle level.

As the Behemoth loped across the room, its foot caught in the snare. Almost immediately, the cable cinched tight.

Thrown off balance, the Behemoth crashed to the ground with such force, the cement floor trembled. Jumping from my hiding spot, I gave a whoop of triumph.

"We did it!" I pumped a fist in the air.

Suddenly, the Behemoth jerked forward onto all fours and lunged at me. The metal cable scraped across the cement floor, sending sparks flying from the friction. The cord. Oh crap, the cord was still long enough to reach me!

I stumbled back against the wall. Nowhere to run. Nowhere to go. As the Behemoth bore down on me, fangs flashing, its snarl was drowned out by the sound of shattering glass. Overhead, the glass ceiling fragmented, sending a cascade of shards raining down.

A dark blur shot down between us, and suddenly the beast was airborne, flung back by a well-placed kick to the face. As it crash-landed, there was a sharp twang of the cable snapping from its mount, accompanied by a more metallic clatter.

Black wings unfurled above my head. Ash landed in front of me, still dressed in the T-shirt and jeans that he'd transformed his original clothing into.

"What took you so long?!" I shouted, wiping long strings of Behemoth drool from my face.

"Is that any way to thank your rescuer?" Ash asked cheerfully, before turning back to the Behemoth. He kicked out of his borrowed sneakers, clearly eager to free his taloned feet.

His clothing burned away in a flood of sparks and soot, revealing the black silk and gold of his original garments.

Twenty feet away, the Behemoth prowled in a cautious half circle, eyeing me the way I'd eye a Double Big Mac. Dark liquid poured down its shoulder, leaving a smatter on the floor.

Blood. It was bleeding. But how was that possible? Had Ash's kick done that much damage?

No. My eyes landed on a golden gleam lying on the cement near the double doors. Whatever artifact had been embedded in the Behemoth's back, it had gotten dislodged when the creature was hurled against the floor.

Before I could draw Ash's attention to the object, the Behemoth rushed at us once more. Ash met it head-on; despite being a pip-squeak of a demon king, his punch packed enough force to stop the beast in its tracks.

"You three get out of here!" he shouted. "I'll take care of this."

Yeah, he could go do that. As Sandra and Carmen ran for the door, I took off after them. Behind me came the crash of colliding bodies and the flapping of wings. Just as I reached the door, Ash cried out, and I looked behind me in time to see him strike the floor. His wings splayed over the cement; the left one was crooked, the feathers snapped and askew.

No. I skidded to a stop. His burning gold eyes met mine from across the room. He bared his teeth, nearly as sharp now as the Behemoth's. Blood unraveled down his chin.

"What did I tell you, human?" he snarled, hoisting himself onto his hands and knees. "Go!"

Yeah, I didn't think so. Cursing my good nature, I rushed back into the room. Closer now, I saw that the golden object that had been dislodged from the Leviathan's shoulder wasn't just a knob—the knob was only the ruby-encrusted pommel of a sword that had been buried to the hilt in the monster's body.

Without thinking, I snatched the sword from the floor. Its handle warmed in my hand, radiating a heat that reminded me of the first time I had used Solomon's ring.

"Zach, come on!" Sandra shouted from the hallway.

I shook my head. "We need to help him!"

The Behemoth grabbed Ash by a broken wing and hauled him from the floor, dangling him in the air like a Barbie doll. From the way he groaned in pain, it dawned on me that when he'd hit the ground, his wing had probably not been the only thing to break.

Gripping the sword in both hands, I rushed at the Behemoth. It threw Ash down and turned to confront me on all fours, one massive hand sweeping downward. I ducked beneath its arm, narrowly avoiding being crushed like a cockroach.

As it swatted at me once more, a crackling ball of light soared overhead and struck it in the face, dissolving into blue sparks. A firecracker. Howling, the creature clawed at its eyes.

Now was my chance! With all my strength, I drove the sword into the monster's flank.

The Behemoth roared in pain and fury. Its scream reverberated through its body with such force, the hilt trembled in my hands. My teeth rattled in my mouth, and my grip quickly weakened.

As my grip began to give way, sparks seethed up the edge of the sword, and the creature's body dissolved into a surge of flames. The Behemoth writhed and raced around the room as the fire continued to spread, before collapsing with such a thud, the ground shuddered. In a matter of seconds, the flames ate away at it until it was reduced to charred bones.

The sword slipped from my numb fingers. Smoke poured from the edge of the blade as the flames winked out.

"Zach!" Sandra and Carmen shouted in unison, rushing to my side.

"I'm fine. Ash—" I turned to him, but he had already risen to his feet. With a gruesome pop, his wing shifted back into place, and the broken feathers crumbled into soot then re-formed whole. Wincing, he wiped at the line of blood inching down his chin and placed a hand over his side. I grimaced at the crack of knitting ribs.

"Don't fret—it would take far more than this to hurt me. I am simply a bit out of practice." His gaze landed on the flaming sword. "Ah, I was wondering where that went. So much like Uriel to pick fights with demons. I suppose he must have lost that one."

"Uriel?" Sandra asked. "You mean the archangel?"

Ash nodded. "Last time I saw him, he was guarding the gates of Eden." He cocked his head, giving it some thought. "I wonder how he's doing now. Probably as annoying as ever."

"The Garden of Eden actually exists?" Carmen asked, her mouth falling open.

He rolled his eyes. "Of course it does. You wouldn't just let your new creations wander around the big world, would you? They're like infants."

I blinked. "So, what you're telling me is that it's basically a giant playpen?"

"Indeed." A smirk touched his lips. "Although these days, I imagine it's not quite as pleasant."

I shook the sword, but the flames continued to surge up the honed metal. "Doesn't this thing have an off button?"

Ash slid his palm along the flat side of the blade. The fire winked out in an instant, wisps of smoke trailing between his clawed fingers. As the light diminished, I caught a trace of sorrow in his gaze. He approached the Behemoth's smoldering carcass.

"Ash, are you all right?" Sandra asked.

He didn't even look at her. "Why wouldn't I be all right?"

"I mean, don't you feel bad? About killing another demon?"

"Death is a human concept," Ash said, before turning back to us. His golden eyes had chilled over in an instant. "The Behemoth is not dead. It is merely asleep once more, regenerating its corporeal body. Only at the end of the world will the beasts of creation find eternal respite."

"You mean die?"

"The Behemoth, Leviathan, and Ziz—it is said their flesh will feed the righteous." A dull smile spread across his lips. "Appetizing, no?"

I groaned. Just the thought of eating the Behemoth made me want to hurl. I'd be spitting up hairballs for weeks.

"What about you?" I asked. "What will happen to you once the world ends?"

For a long moment, he didn't answer. Then he chuckled. "A fate just as terrible."

It dawned on me that Ash had just as much to lose in this fight as the rest of the world. I thought that as a demon, he could do anything, but his fate had already been decided for him. Maybe, like Frankenstein's monster, it had been decided even before he'd been created.

"So that's why you're helping us?" I asked. "Because you don't want to die."

"This world is much too interesting to be destroyed," he said, huffing. "I can assure you, death is the thing I'm least afraid of."

As he looked back at the Behemoth's remains, his smile faded by a degree, and he nudged one of the charred chunks with his clawed foot.

"I don't mind it, being here," he added, retrieving his borrowed sneakers from where he'd kicked them into the corner. "Despite your shortcomings, you humans have your benefits. Pizza, for example, and those delicious rainbow circles we ate at the theater."

"M&M's," Sandra said.

He pointed a finger at her. "Exactly. You try living on a few thousand years of manna. It gets old fast."

"Unless we can stop this thing, I don't think we'll be around for another year, much less a thousand," I said.

"So pessimistic," Sandra said. "One down, two more to go."

"On top of the Knights of the Apocalypse," I added as we began the long walk back to town.

24

THE MOMENT I returned home from school three days later, I traded out my backpack for the gym bag I'd stowed under my bed. Padded in a beach towel within the bag, Uriel's sword radiated a soft, unnatural heat as I traced my fingers down its blade. I tilted the sword to catch the sun, admiring the way the light shimmered down its length, the polished steel glowing reddish gold like the memory of fire.

Each day after school, Carmen would drive us to the beach in her mom's old Volkswagen, where we would sit until dinnertime, swimming or playing volleyball, but mostly just waiting. Ash was convinced that the Leviathan would be the next monster to awaken, and just as the Behemoth had crawled from the earth, the Leviathan would rise from the sea.

As for the explosion at the abandoned factory, it was probably the most interesting thing that had happened in San Pancras's entire history, and for the first day or two after, reporters had flooded the streets. Even my cousin Samantha got excited about it and drove out to the crevice to film another video.

Luckily, no one had yet wised up to the fact that our small town was the site of the apocalypse. My dad thought an old cache of chemicals must've gotten ignited somehow, while my science teacher, Mrs. Tucker, dismissed the Behemoth's destruction as the result of a very small-scale earthquake that had been limited to the town's confines. The only victim was Carmen's beloved Buick, which had disappeared into the bottomless depths of the earth.

Word around school was that some big-deal scientists had come to test the soil and take measurements of the fissures left in the Behemoth's wake. Sandra said they'd even bagged up the Buick's broken-off side mirror. I had expected them to uncover charred chunks of flesh and bone, but by the sound of it, the scientists had left mystified, and not a trace of the creature remained. When I told Ash this, he simply shrugged.

"Why would there be a corpse for something that cannot be killed?" he had said nonchalantly. "From dust we are made, and to dust we will return. The Behemoth will simply dream beneath the earth until it is awakened once more."

There was something almost sad about the way he had said it, and in the moments before he turned away, a shadow passed over his face. Some remnant of sorrow.

I gulped. "Do you mean they can summon it again?"

"Yes, although it will take five days for the Behemoth's body to re-form. I imagine that in the meanwhile, the Knights of the Apocalypse will work on awakening the Leviathan."

Worry hung over me like a dark cloud as I packed my swim trunks and spare T-shirt in the duffel bag, padding them carefully over the sword. Unless we could find the Knights of the Apocalypse first, it would only be a matter of time before the next beast was summoned. But what if it wasn't the Leviathan at all like Ash thought? What if the Ziz appeared instead, when we were at the beach, and we weren't prepared for it?

There was nothing I could do about that, so I decided to focus on something I could prevent—skin cancer. As I looked around for the sunscreen, my mom marched Naomi into the bedroom and deposited her on my bed.

"You're taking your sister to the beach today," Mom announced, strict and no-nonsense.

I gulped. "But, Mom, I'm going out with my friends. If I take her, I'll be the only one who has to bring their little sister along."

"That's what older siblings are for, Zach. You watch out for each other and take care of each other. No buts—just do it or I won't let you go at all."

I groaned. When Mom worded it that way, I didn't have much of a choice. The moment she left the room, I turned to Naomi. The little brat wiped the tears from her cheeks and gave me a satisfied smirk.

"What did you tell Mom?" I asked, narrowing my eyes at her.

She confronted me with her chin raised, giving an almost eerie Mom impression. "I know that you're doing something fun without me, Zach."

"We're just going to the beach. I thought you hated it there.

Remember last time you went? You thought the sand was gross and the seaweed stank. Why do you even want to go?"

"This has something to do with the magical ring, doesn't it?" Naomi crossed her arms. "It wasn't stolen after all. You just want to talk to sharks on your own."

"It has nothing to do with that, and for your information, the ring *was* stolen. Besides, I already summoned a gullnado, and I have no intention of making a shark one! I've seen the movies, so I know how that turns out. Now tell Mom you're going to stay home and play with your toys."

"I don't think so." She shook her head. "You heard what she said—either I come too, or you don't go at all."

I wanted to scream. Little sisters could be so frustrating, and Naomi was doubly so. Taking a deep breath, I raked a hand through my hair.

"Fine, it does have to do with the ring, but it's not that we have it. This secret society called the Knights of the Apocalypse took it, Naomi. We're going to the beach because we think they're going to do something evil with it there. It's not safe for you to go. You'll just get hurt. Trust me."

"I'm going or neither of us are," she said with the kind of aggravating self-confidence of someone who always knew how to get her way. She was basically the evil mastermind of our family, and it was a mystery to me who she got it from. Dad couldn't plot his way out of a paper bag, and the only tyranny Mom had committed was making us clean our rooms.

Sighing, I relented. "All right, fine. But if something happens, you have to promise me you'll run and find somewhere safe to hide before the monster gets you. Because, uh, I'm pretty sure it'll eat you. Like a French fry."

I expected her to bail and change her mind, but instead she just smiled cheerfully. "I promise."

As I waited for Naomi to gather her stuff, I texted Sandra to give her a head's up that we'd gotten stuck with babysitter duty. She responded seconds later: What?!

I told her the reason why, and even though the typing icon appeared for a minute afterward, she didn't get back to me. Sighing, I followed Naomi out to the front yard and leaned against the tree as we waited for Carmen to drive up.

"So, what kind of monster is it?" Naomi asked.

"A really scary one, probably with a lot of teeth. Apparently, it lives beneath the ocean, and these evil men are gonna try to use the ring to awaken it. We're going to stop them."

"How?"

Taking a wary glance around the street, I leaned down and unzipped my duffel bag. I gently parted the towels to reveal the silvery gleam of Uriel's sword. When my fingertips stroked the metal, its warmth radiated through my palm.

As I told Naomi about what had happened with the Behemoth, she listened gravely. She had always been mature for her age, like a cranky wizard trapped in a nine-year-old body. When she had been one or two, she had barely even screamed or shouted, instead latching stubbornly on to my mom's arm and glowering at me through her flaxen hair.

Ten minutes later, Sandra and Carmen pulled up. Ash was sprawled out in the back seat, and with a resentful look in our direction, slid out of the way and leaned against the car door to give Naomi and me room to sit down.

"What's she doing here?" he asked, eyeing Naomi.

She turned to me. "Who's this?"

"He's the guardian of the ring," I said awkwardly.

"Ashmedai, king of demons," Ash said, although with none of his usual vigor. Ever since we had defeated the Behemoth, he had seemed moody and distracted. I thought it must be about being so close to the water, that the scent of fish and sea brine must be nauseating to him, but I wasn't so sure.

Naomi took this news rather well, nodding and staring at him until her unwavering gaze forced him to look away. I blinked. It appeared even the king of demons was capable of being intimidated by Naomi's death stare.

The drive to the beach was short and uneventful. Carmen rolled down the windows and whistled along to video game or anime soundtracks on her iPhone, and Ash finished the hamburger she had bought for him in solemn silence, not even appearing to really enjoy it.

"Is something wrong?" I asked him.

"No, I've just been remembering lately."

"Remembering what?"

"What came before. Everything's been coming back slowly, year by year."

"Well, that can't be too bad, right?"

His expression was grave. "I think that the last time I was awakened, the Knights of the Apocalypse tried to use the ring. They were stopped then as well, but the result was terrible.

The amount of people whose lives were ruined because of it…" He trailed off.

For a demon, it struck me how much he seemed to care about the earth's survival and about the people on it. I wanted to believe that his feelings were genuine and he wasn't just putting on a guise for our benefit.

"We won't let that happen this time," Sandra said, and Carmen nodded in agreement.

"Yeah," I said, taking him by the shoulder. "This time, we'll bring the Knights down for good. We'll get them all thrown in jail, or at least humiliate them enough that they won't try again."

He smiled thinly. "Yeah."

But even as he turned away, the strain in his features remained, and only tightened as we drew closer to the beach. I didn't want to ask him what he remembered. I knew from the pictures we had found online that it must have been something truly horrifying. All this time, I had found a strange comfort in the savagery of monsters, and I was beginning to realize that what drew me to scary movies in the first place was how predictable they were. The monster always came back for a second scare. The jock was one of the first victims to die. And in almost all of the movies, there was a final girl, the sole survivor, the one who prevailed because she was supposed to represent goodness or compassion.

But that wasn't how it worked in the real world. Sometimes, there were no survivors. Sometimes, the villains won. And the true monsters didn't wear masks. They could be friendly. They could smile at you and seem like someone you could trust.

These thoughts lingered in my head as I helped Sandra set up the beach umbrella while Carmen took Naomi to the dressing rooms to change into her swimsuit and rent a floaty. The cheery glint of the sunlight across the water couldn't stir the unease that settled over me.

Sinking my feet in the surf, I closed my eyes and leaned back, trying to get comfortable. I craned my head to the sky. The sun warmed my face, balmy and familiar.

Sandra gripped my arm suddenly. "Zach!"

"What is it?" Rising to my feet, I searched the still water for any sign of disturbance. Then I realized her gaze was focused on something to the right of us, still on the beach.

A familiar voice said, "Hey, birdbrain!"

Oh, great. Team Neanderthal had arrived. I turned to confront Jeffrey and his lackeys, and felt my stomach drop as I glimpsed a new face in the crowd. Dominic stood right next to Jeffrey, smirking with all the rest.

I felt as if someone had punched me in the stomach, and then had taken a shot lower just as a bonus. I had seen Dominic hanging around with some of Jeffrey's friends before, but I had thought nothing of it and told myself it was only because they were both on the baseball team. This was worse than being attacked by seagulls, and even worse than that time in fourth grade when I'd accidentally called our teacher Mom. It felt personal.

"What are you doing here, Jeffrey?" Sandra asked dryly.

"Shouldn't you be out scrounging through garbage or kicking puppies?"

"Look, he needs a girl to defend him," Dominic said, and Jeffrey laughed and gave him a high five.

The fluttery feeling in my stomach that came whenever I glanced in Dominic's direction disappeared in an instant, as if Jeffrey had trampled the butterflies beneath his elephant feet. I bit my inner cheek, choking down the heavy lump that built in my throat. Why had I ever thought Dominic and I could be friends, or that he might ever like someone like me? We were nothing alike. Seriously, he didn't even like werewolf movies!

"We were just out on my dad's boat," Jeffrey said with a grin, jangling a pair of keys in my face. "Too bad you guys are so lame that all you can do is to sit here underneath that stupid umbrella."

I doubted that Jeffrey was allowed to drive the boat on his own. He was probably just holding the keys for his dad until the guy returned, but it still felt like an insult anyway. I would've liked to take those keys and shove them down his throat. Instead, all I could do was just stand there, tongue-tied.

I stared at Dominic. His smile faded, and he began looking a bit uneasy, like he thought I might lunge at him.

I don't need you, I thought. *I never needed you.*

"They probably just came across each other here, Zach," Sandra said with a small consolatory smile as Jeffrey and his friends continued down the beach in the direction of the food stands. "They don't even like the same things. And I don't think Jeffrey is—"

"Don't even say it," I said tightly. "If you say it, it will turn me straight."

Jeffrey glanced back over his shoulder. Our eyes met, and he gave me a smile, only not a friendly one. It was basically the smile every actor who played a supervillain in the movies had to ace before landing the role—that cruel little half sneer that would've typecast him as Slappy from *Goosebumps*, if he'd been short enough to play a murderous ventriloquist dummy.

Not good.

The only time he smiled at me like that was when he was plotting something truly evil, like the time he had put worms in my desk in third grade, or when he more recently decided to perfect his aim by throwing loose change at me.

I began to shy away, but something kept me riveted to him. The unease that prickled down my spine was sharpened by an edge of anger, and before I knew it, I felt my nails nip into my palms. All this time, I had cowered from Jeffrey, afraid of his cruel words, hurled coins, shoves, and punches. I was so sick of standing down and just letting him do whatever he wanted to me.

I had fought the Behemoth. I didn't need a magic ring or a flaming sword to stand up to him.

"Where are you going, Zach?" Sandra asked as I stepped toward Jeffrey and the others.

"Payback," I growled through gritted teeth. Nothing would ever change unless I made it.

"Are you crazy?" She grabbed me by the wrist. "He's there with his entire gang, and we have more important things to worry about right now. Carmen and your sister are going to be back any minute."

"Don't you get it, Sandra?" I ripped my hand free and swiveled around to face her. "If I don't do something, he's going to harass us forever. He's never going to stop."

This time, as I began walking, she didn't stop me. Jeffrey and the others had turned their attention back ahead and were making their way to the hotdog stand.

"Hey, Jeffrey!"

Jeffrey turned around to face me, his nostrils flared like a dog catching a whiff of kibble. His wicked smile was gone, and it took him a moment to find it again, only this time there was a trace of unease there. His blue eyes were chilled by wariness. The bullied never approached the bully. It went against the natural order, like cats barking and fish flying.

"I might be a birdbrain, but at least I'm not a coward like you," I shouted, and the rest of the boys turned toward me.

"Excuse me?" he asked, narrowing his eyes. "What did you just call me?"

"I don't need to hide behind a pack of goons or pick on kids smaller than me. And unlike you, I didn't run away at the zoo. You know what? I'll bet you peed yourself that day too. I think I even caught a whiff of it."

His face flushed crimson. "You'd better shut up right now."

"Or what?" I stepped even closer. "Too embarrassed for your friends to know what a pants-peeing coward you are?"

"That's it!" He lunged at me, drawing back his arm to strike me. I raised my arms to block him, but apparently defeating the

Behemoth hadn't given me superpowers—or good reflexes, for that matter—because seconds later, he drove his fist into my stomach. I staggered back, my lungs seizing shut. Ugh, it felt like he'd punched a hole through my gut.

What had I been hoping for? It wasn't like this was a horror movie, and even if it had been one, I'd probably be the first to be killed by Zombie Jeffrey or Vampire Jeffrey.

As Jeffrey wheeled his fist at me, I swung my leg out to kick him. My sandal glanced pathetically off his thigh—and he was thrown back five feet by the force of the blow.

No way. My mouth fell open as he rolled across the sand, before coming to a stop in front of Dominic and the others, whose smirks had faded into befuddled gapes. Had I done that?

Maybe getting splattered with Behemoth drool had given me powers after all, like Spider-Man's radioactive spider bite, only much nastier.

Jeffrey lurched to his feet, spitting out sand. The fury blazing in his eyes burned even brighter. A thin line of blood inched from his nostril, and he swatted the droplets away, drawing a crimson smear across his face like war paint. "You're gonna regret that."

So, this was how Pokémon felt when they evolved. I grinned. "Bring it on."

Bellowing, he rushed at me and tackled me to the ground. It hurt as much as usual, but this time, I had a bit of magic on my side. I shoved him hard in the chest, and he flew back as though wrenched, landing in the waves a good eight feet offshore.

As I rose to my feet, Jeffrey emerged from the surf, sputtering in outrage. The other members of his Sasquatch Squad bailed, not even giving him a chance to wade to shore. I sighed as Dominic ran after them, though not before he cast a fearful look my way, like he thought I might transform into a werewolf at any moment. I was half-tempted to howl after him.

All this time, I had wanted to be Dominic's friend, but I hadn't known him at all. I had just liked his straight brown hair, and the freckles splayed across his cheeks, and his bright blue eyes. But deep down, he was no different than the rest of them.

I returned to Sandra, who was watching from a distance with a blank look of shock.

"Did you see that?" I couldn't help but grin. "Jeffrey's never gonna mess with me again, now that I have superpowers."

She took a deep breath. "Zach…"

"Where's Ash?"

Hot breath brushed against the nape of my neck. "You can say thank you."

I swiveled around. Though I couldn't see Ash, I felt the dry scrape of his feathers when I reached out and patted the empty air in front of me. "W-wait, don't tell me, it was *you*?"

"Don't sound so upset." Ash winked into view once we returned to our beach umbrella. "Wasn't this what you wanted?"

"Well, yeah, but…"

I was about to say more when a strange tremor passed down my spine, and I heard the scrape of sand sluicing through the water. I looked down, stunned to see grains of sand flowing outward, into the waves, although there was no water to the draw them in.

I exchanged look with the others. "Is that what I think it is?"

"The Leviathan," Ash murmured.

"Where?" I searched the placid water, goosebumps prickling up my arms. "I don't see it anywhere. What exactly are we looking for?"

"The sand is going out to sea," Sandra pointed out. "It's gotta be offshore."

"W-wait, are you telling me that we have to face that thing on the open water?" I stammered. As this if this couldn't get any worse. We had faced the Behemoth on solid ground, and it had still managed to nearly kill me! This time, I'd probably lose a limb if I had to stand down a monster in the sea, or at least inadvertently re-create scenes from *Jaws*. "How are we even supposed to get out there? It's not as if you can fly all three of us, right?"

Ash grinned, his gaze straying to where Jeffrey was sulking by his friends, drenched from his dip in the water. "A boat certainly would help, wouldn't you agree?"

I groaned. "Oh, no. Please tell me you're not thinking of stealing one."

"I prefer to think of it as borrowing," he said, and winked out of sight again.

25

OMINOUS STORM CLOUDS rolled in from offshore, and a harsh wind picked up. Scrunches of paper and plastic wrappers tumbled over our sandaled feet as Sandra and I hurried down the boardwalk.

"You know, I'm beginning to think you're right, Sandra."

She glanced over at me as we passed luxurious yachts. "Right about what?"

"Ash is definitely trying to damn me to hell, if there is a hell. Souls probably taste better once they've been cooked in fire and brimstone for a while."

She rolled her eyes, turning back ahead. "Luckily, I don't think stealing is enough to get you sent there."

"Not even a boat?" I grinned. "That's gonna at least get me sent to the sixth circle."

Joking made me feel better. Just a little. But it was hard to keep the humor flowing when the sky grew darker with each passing moment as the storm clouds spread across the sky. Hats and litter tumbled in a sharp breeze, and the waves below thrashed against the wooden stilts of the dock. Already, most of the beachgoers were packing up their things.

Naomi took forever to get dressed when our parents dragged us out to eat, but I knew changing into her swimsuit didn't take *this* long. By now she and Carmen would've almost certainly finished their business at the floaty rental and returned to the beach. I was afraid to look back and spot them searching for us, or worse—Jeffrey in swift pursuit, flanked by an entire police squadron. When I finally worked up the courage to glance over my shoulder, I was relieved to find the marina deserted.

I scanned the rows of vessels, searching for something that would match Jeffrey's personality. The boat would probably have spikes studding the prow and sides, along with nets containing the sorry remains of missing pets and children. But as we continued down the dock and purplish-black thunderheads brewed overhead, our search began to seem hopeless. We'd never find the boat at this rate. And if we waited here much longer, we'd probably end up behind bars. Cafeteria food was nasty enough—I imagined prison food would be so disgusting, it'd make even Ash think twice before taking a bite.

No sooner had the thought crossed my mind than I spotted a boat at the end of the row, a sleek white vessel about thirty feet long with a covered cockpit. Emblazoned in gold on its side was the name *Cooper's Glory.* I scoffed. That was so like him—or his dad at least—to name the boat after his own last name.

"That's it," Sandra and I said in unison, and a metallic jangle rose from behind us. I turned around. The key ring Jeffrey had flashed at us mockingly now bobbed in thin air.

Ash winked into existence like a light bulb flipped on, grinning. "What are you two waiting for? Get on."

He seemed even more intense than before, as if using his powers had ignited the uncontrollable power I'd sensed within him. Or maybe it was the approaching beast. Maybe as a kindred demon, something about the Leviathan resonated with him.

Just as we boarded the vessel, a pair of figures raced down the boardwalk. My heart dropped as I caught sight of Carmen and Naomi. Oh, great. This was even worse than if Jeffrey had confronted us.

"What are you three doing?" Carmen shouted, apparently eager to get us all arrested. Beside me, Sandra groaned.

"Zach, wait for me," Naomi hollered. "Don't leave without me."

I rolled my eyes. Right, because God forbid she missed out on this exciting near-death experience.

"Hurry up," I said, turning to Ash. "Start the boat, before they get any closer!"

"Hey, I know you three can hear me!" Trying to catch our attention, Carmen waved the rented dolphin floaty in the air like one of those walking-advertisement people who twirled signs at street corners. A powerful gust of wind blew the floaty from her hands and sent it tumbling into the water.

Ash looked blankly at the keys. I realized how stupid it was to depend on a demon to commit grand theft auto. Lunging over to the steering wheel, I grabbed the keys from his hand and stuck them into the ignition, as I had seen Carmen do with her car. After a moment or two of struggling to no avail, Sandra cleared her throat and held out her hand expectantly.

"Let me give it a try," she said, favoring me with a confident smile. I pass the keys over and made a beeline for the railing just as Carmen skidded to a stop on the dock in front of us.

"You'd better get your butt out here this instant, Sandra," Carmen said, pushing up her glasses, which had fallen sideways during her frantic run. "Leviathan or not, stealing a boat is going too far. We already wrecked my car for the cause!"

"If we don't steal boats, there won't be any boats left by the time this creature gets on land," I pointed out.

She gave it more thought. "That's true, but—"

From behind me came the rumble of the engine turning on. Sandra gave a victorious whoop.

"Sorry, Carmen," I called as the boat pulled away from the dock. "We'll bring it back, don't worry."

She shook her fist at us and exhausted enough swear words to make even a drunken sailor blush. I didn't realize something was wrong until we were well offshore, and suddenly it dawned on me that Carmen was standing alone on the dock. Where was Naomi?

"Mom's going to be so furious," Naomi said, and I pivoted around to find her grinning at me in utter delight.

I sputtered for a response, but all I could manage was a stuttering, "How...? When?"

"You two were so busy yelling at Carmen, even an elephant could've sneaked on here." She rolled her eyes, sitting down on the wooden bench at the boat's prow.

I turned to Ash, my face heating up. "I can't believe you. How could you just let her sneak on?"

"Don't blame me," he said, scowling. "She's your sister after all."

"You have to fly her back to shore. She can't be here."

"I can take care of myself just fine," she insisted as we coasted farther offshore.

"First of all, Naomi, you're nine. Second, you weren't even able to handle a gullnado!"

"Well, neither were you," she pointed out, pouting.

"That doesn't matter. The point is, you're just going to get in the way!" As my voice rose in desperation, it decided in that inopportune moment to crack. Wonderful. Clearing my throat, I tried again. "How am I supposed to protect you on a boat?"

"You don't have to protect me. I'll be just fine!"

I groaned. Why did she have to be so stubborn?

As I returned to Sandra's side, my gaze was drawn to an object bolted on the cockpit's wall, right beside the steering wheel. With its metal barrel, it almost looked like...

"Is that a *rifle*?" I blurted, and the others looked in my direction.

"Only one way to find out!" Naomi said with a wicked grin, and I blocked her with my arm before she could get close. No way was I letting a nine-year-old touch a deadly weapon.

"It looks like a harpoon gun," Sandra said.

"Do you know how to use one?"

"No." She gave it some thought. "But I mean, it can't be *too* hard, right?"

I rolled my eyes. "Yeah, if you want to shoot yourself in the foot."

By now, the shore was just a thin strip on the horizon. The farther we got from land, the more restless the sea became. Less than an hour before, the sky had been a clear blue, without a cloud in sight, but now it was nearly pitch-black, and thunder rumbled overhead. This wasn't good. The Behemoth had only caused a minor earthquake, but this looked like it was about to become the storm of the century.

"Where'd you learn how to steer a boat?" I asked Sandra.

"My uncle has a fishing boat he takes us out on sometimes. It isn't as nice as this one, but the steering is the same at least. I think."

Yeah, I didn't like the sound of that.

There were several life vests hanging from the railing, and I helped Naomi into one before finding another that fit me. After Sandra had gotten hers on, there was still one left for Ash, but he scoffed and shook his head when I explained the ridiculous-looking garment's purpose.

"I appreciate your concern, but unlike you mortals, if I fall into the water, I can simply fly out," he said, rolling his eyes. "In any case, I wouldn't be caught dead wearing something like that. I'd rather drown."

"That's easy for you to say when you're immortal," I pointed out, and he shrugged.

"Yes, walking the earth for a couple thousand years does give you a remarkable sense of style and fashion."

"Which is apparently why you still dress as if you're in ancient Egypt."

"Ancient Jerusalem, but close enough."

"You don't *look* like a demon," Naomi said, peering at him suspiciously.

"King of demons," he corrected.

As we headed farther out from shore, the more tumultuous the sea became. Waves thrashed against the metal hull of the boat, spraying me in the face with salty foam. I grabbed on to the railing tightly, wishing that *Jaws* hadn't been one of the first horror movies I'd seen, not to mention the only one that still terrified me. All of a sudden, I was pretty sure we did, in fact, need a bigger boat.

Across from me, Sandra groaned and settled against the railing, her face ripening to shades of green. "Do you have a bucket?" she asked as I took control of the wheel. "I think I'm going to—"

She leaned over the railing. I grimaced at the splash of her lunch striking the side of the boat.

After wiping her mouth, she settled down again, shaking her head. "Why couldn't it be a giant bird? A unicorn. I don't know."

"The bird comes last," Ash said with a grim smile. "Although, I intend to get the ring back before it comes to that."

Sandra groaned a second time.

"Oh yeah, we have one more after this, don't we? I'm beginning to think it might be best just to let someone else deal with this, like Superman." She gave it more thought. "Or maybe the coast guard should be alerted. Don't they know how to deal with this stuff?"

"I don't think the army trains soldiers how to fight monsters," Naomi piped up helpfully.

"No, instead, all we have is a magical sword, a harpoon gun, an obnoxious nine-year-old—"

"Hey!" she said.

"—and the king of demons," I finished, before turning my attention back to steering the boat. "I think I'd prefer one of those warships right now."

"I can assure you, my powers are more than enough to take down that measly tadpole," Ash boasted.

"Remind me, how helpful were you against the Behemoth?" I pointed out. "It nearly killed you."

He scoffed. "Yes, well, you'd be a bit out of practice too after sleeping for a few hundred years."

A faint, growing warmth spread through my duffel bag, grabbing my attention.

"Hey, Sandra, take the wheel again," I said, and once she did, I rested the bag on the deck. As I unzipped it, streams of smoke wisped between my fingers. No sooner did my fingers curl around the sword's hilt than a streak of fire radiated up the blade, engulfing it from guard to tip.

I groaned, waving the sword around in an effort to staunch the flames. "Not again."

Suddenly, Ash rose to his feet, his eyes seething with golden light. A slow smile spread across his face, revealing the needle-sharp points of his teeth. "It's coming."

Sandra twisted the key, turning off the engine. A meager puff of black smoke spit from the exhaust pipe. As the boat bobbed in the surf, I searched the unsettled waves, clenching the railing in a white-knuckled grip.

As I looked back to shore, it shocked me how far away the land seemed, just a thin crust of sand upon the horizon. Once the boat's shuddering had stilled, my fingers strayed to my life vest. Something told me I should've brought a suit of armor instead.

Sandra retrieved the harpoon gun from the wall, fumbling with the triple-barbed harpoons in the plastic case below it. I stepped out of her way as she tried loading the weapon. I had seen enough horror movies to know that if something could go wrong, it probably would. And in this case, end with me being shish-kebabed.

"Do you see the Leviathan?" Sandra asked.

"No, but I feel it getting closer," Ash said, his clothing dissolving into a flood of black silk and feathers. My stomach twisted into knots. Something about him seemed different this time, as if the air around him was distorting, bending like light through a prism. He was becoming stronger, or maybe just coming back in tune with the power hidden inside himself.

The sea had gone still. Beneath the surface, I caught glimpses of shadowy forms—dolphins and sharks and entire schools of fish fleeing toward the shoreline. They had the right idea.

"It's just a giant fish," I whispered to myself, tightening my hold on the sword. "It can't hurt you. It's just a big fish. A goldfish. Think of it that way."

The sea went dead still, and my tensed muscles slowly relaxed. Then the boat began to tip back as the ocean's surface swelled, as if a massive form had passed beneath us. I held on to the railing to keep from falling.

"Don't you dare let us drown, demon!" Sandra shouted, clinging to the railing with one hand as Ash took flight.

"What was that?" he called back earnestly, finding a perch on the cockpit's roof. "I'm afraid I didn't catch that."

Before she could say more, a massive serpent-like form broke the surface no more than thirty feet away. It lashed through the water, its back ridged with spikes.

I took a deep breath. Okay, that wasn't so bad. It was about fifteen feet long. We could deal with that.

My stomach plummeted as the sea serpent surfaced—not a head bristling with teeth, but an anchor-shaped fin lined on either side with jagged spines.

That wasn't the Leviathan at all.

It was only its tail.

26

ON SECOND THOUGHT, running away sounded like a pretty good idea.

"Sandra, get us out of here!" I said, but she was already revving the engine. The boat lurched forward, spewing sea-foam in the air and making my stomach do flip-flops.

Behind us, the Leviathan vanished beneath the surface, leaving a trail of ripples in its wake. I glimpsed it through the water, its silver scales gleaming. I wondered if this was the source of all those legends—the Loch Ness monster, the Hydra, and others.

I had never thought that I would end up in this situation. No more flea markets for me, I swore. No more magical rings, no more making friends with demons. After this, I'd devote the rest of my life to peacefully living in a cave somewhere. If I survived, that is.

The Leviathan's tail lashed out of the water. Its fin screeched across the boat's glistening metal hull, scraping out the Cooper name embellished in gold along its side.

"No way," I whispered.

"Zach, I've changed my mind," Naomi whimpered, on the verge of tears. She tugged at my sleeve. "I want to go home. I don't want to fight the sea monster."

"Don't worry, you don't have to fight it," I said, grasping her shoulder firmly. I twisted toward Sandra. "Can we make this boat go any faster?" My own voice rose frantically.

"I'm trying," Sandra cried, the blood draining from her face.

"Well, try harder!"

She turned to face me. "Would you like to give this a try, Zach? Be my guest."

Well, when she worded it like that... I backed away to give her some space to concentrate. She worked the levers and buttons desperately, and the boat steadily picked up speed.

"I have a feeling running will just make the Leviathan hungrier," Ash said helpfully, jumping down from the cockpit's roof. I shot a glare his way. As far as I was concerned, we should at least make the demon work for its meal.

"Do you see the Leviathan, Naomi?" I asked.

Naomi shook her head, her face dead white. Tightening the hold around the sword, I searched the restless water.

"This is the last time I'm listening to you, Zach!" Sandra said. "I told you, but you wouldn't listen. You should've just taken the ring to a priest or a rabbi."

"Well, excuse me," I snapped back. "Don't blame me. Blame

the people who summoned this thing, or blame Ash for letting them take the ring in the first place so he could get *pizza*!"

"Of course, let's blame the demon," Ash said, rolling his eyes. "How typical."

As I was about to say more, the water beneath us welled up and the boat began to tip. With a cry, I stumbled back against the railing. Naomi screamed out, and Sandra said something in Spanish that I had a feeling her mother wouldn't approve of. Even Ash grabbed hold of the railing. Thirty feet away or so, the creature's tail flapped through the restless waves, and down past the boat's railing, almost directly below us, I caught a glimpse of two glowing gold disks passing underwater. They looked like headlights, except...

It dawned on me. Those were its eyes.

Before I could cry out and warn Sandra, the Leviathan had already slipped out of sight into the dark water, thrashing the sea-foam into white mounds. Frantically, I wheeled around, searching for any sign of the beast as Sandra steered the boat toward the marina. But it had disappeared once more into the depths.

"Not toward shore!" I shouted over the howling wind. A few fat raindrops plopped onto the deck, and by the look of it, it would start pouring any second. "If we lure it toward shore, it'll hurt people."

"Zach, I'm not exactly prepared to be eaten," Sandra yelled back, and was about to say more when the boat made a gargled groan. Uh-oh, that didn't sound good. Black smoke spit from the exhaust pipe, and the boat slowly slowed to a halt.

I hurried to Sandra's side with Naomi nearly clinging to my leg. "What's wrong with it?"

"I don't know." Frantically, she yanked at the levers. "I think it's out of gas."

"Can't you do something?!"

"Like what, Zach?" she snapped. "Do I look like the gas fairy to you?"

Overhead, a bolt of lightning streaked across the sky, and then a second bolt zigzagged down and touched the waves nearby. Steam fizzled from the water's surface, and although the Leviathan continued to circle us, other smaller fish floated dead to the surface and fingers of electricity crawled up the side of the boat. I yanked Naomi away from the railing, the hairs rising on the nape of my neck. Even Ash's feathers ruffled up a bit where he stood at the opposite end of the deck.

If one of those bolts touched us, forget about becoming fish bait. The Leviathan would end up with a deep-fried special instead of its usual raw-meat meal.

"Seriously?" I shouted at Ash. "We have to deal with a storm now too?"

"If you think this is bad, wait until the end of the world," he said grimly.

As raindrops cascaded down, the sea's surface swelled beneath us once more. This time, the boat didn't just rock, but began leaning sideways. The Leviathan's tail lashed through the water, coming so close to us that I felt it cut the air.

"Naomi, don't let go of that!" I said as she gripped on to the captain's seat. Rain lashed down around us, and wind tore at the sides of the boat.

The vessel tilted, waves lapping at its hull like hungry mouths. My grip failed on the sword as I clung to the railing. Skidding down the deck in a silver flash, the blade left a trail of sparks in its wake.

"Ash, grab the sword," I shouted, but he had already taken flight. Of course. He didn't have to worry about drowning when he could just fly back to shore.

The monstrous tail sank back under the surface, sending high waves crashing against the boat. The force of the waves drove me to my knees and nearly threw Naomi overboard.

"Zach, don't you dare let me drown," she shouted. "If you do, I'll tell Mom!"

"Naomi, I hate to break it to you, but you can't tell Mom if you're dead! Just hold on and stay away from the railing." Twisting onto my back, I blinked raindrops from my eyes and searched the deck for a glimpse of fire or honed steel. If the sword had fallen overboard, I'd eat my own shoe.

"I hate fish," Ash said with a grimace, landing on the deck. "They stink and they don't even taste good, except for when they're on pizza. See, this is why I can't have a good sibling relationship."

If that was his sibling, I hated to see who his parents were. Maybe all demons saw themselves as one big happy family. I could just imagine the game nights.

Even now, my mouth had a mind of its own, and as the boat

continued shaking, I blabbed out, "You must be the baby of the family."

At the very least, I figured Ash would cheat at Monopoly as shamelessly as Naomi did.

"You should know better than to make assumptions about a person's height," he said, shooting me a glare scalding enough to melt steel.

As the boat stopped tilting, I stumbled to my feet. "Ash, do you see the sword?"

He looked around, clearly befuddled. "Weren't you holding it?"

Ugh, he could be so frustrating! For the king of demons, he was about as smart as a sack of potatoes. Scrambling over the slippery boards, I searched desperately for the sword.

"Zach, over there!" Naomi said and pointed across the deck. A flash of steel caught my eye.

Quick as a striking rattler, the Leviathan lunged forward, its smooth silver body rippling through the storm-gray water. I snagged the sword just as the beast reached us, raising the blade only to find myself confronted by an empty space where the Leviathan had been mere seconds before.

The boat rocked and shuddered as the water rose around us, displaced by the Leviathan's moving body. Sandra and Naomi staggered to one end of the vessel and I to the other, and Ash took flight, circling around us.

Where were the fireballs or lightning strikes? Talk about underrated!

Sandra aimed the harpoon gun at the monster and pulled

the trigger. The harpoon whizzed through the air, missing it by a good ten feet.

"Sandra!" I groaned.

"Excuse me," she snapped back, reloading the gun. "I've seen you in gym, Zach. You're an even worse aim than I am!"

She had a point. I turned to Ash. "Can't you do anything?"

"I can't," he admitted, landing on the railing.

My mouth dropped open. "Wait, a minute. You *can't*?!"

"As long as I'm in this wretched form, I can only channel a minuscule amount of my true power," he explained through clenched teeth. Each word came out strained and forceful. "I'm stuck like this."

"Why couldn't you have told us this before?" I demanded.

"I didn't think it was important."

"You—"

Before I could finish, the Leviathan burst from the ocean mere feet from the boat. Its head was a bulbous mass of silvery-gray flesh lined with a nestful of needle-sharp teeth, its whirling round eyes as bright as lanterns. A glowing orb hung from a stalk on its forehead, reminding me of an anglerfish's lure.

In a blur of spines and scales, it coiled around the boat like a snake strangling a mouse, the railing bending beneath its muscular tail. The boat shuddered in its grasp, tilting so violently to the side, I feared we would be cast into the water. I darted to the side, sliding beneath the Leviathan's head as it lunged toward me, jaws wide open. Hundreds of fangs brimmed from its cavernous mouth.

The monster's breath rushed over me in a hot wave, making me gag on the nauseating reek of rotting fish. It would have been enough to knock out any ordinary person, but Ash actually staggered back as though struck, losing a few feet of altitude in the process and coming to a crash-landing on the deck.

"Aim for its head," Ash shouted, lurching onto his hands and knees. "The light is the center of power."

The Leviathan rippled across the deck, making a beeline for where Naomi cowered against the captain's seat, sobbing uncontrollably. I raced forward, nearly sliding across the rain-drenched boards. I barely felt my legs beneath me, and my vision narrowed until the only thing left was her tear-streaked face and that monstrous thing surging straight toward her.

I took a running leap, aiming for the glowing bulb that bobbed from a slender stalk in the middle of the Leviathan's forehead. My aim fell short, and I plunged the flaming sword into its neck instead, high enough up that my toes barely scraped the floor. The blade cut effortlessly through the scales and flesh, and I was met by a brittle snap as it cracked the bone beneath.

I expected the Leviathan to go limp, maybe spew out coins like in a video game, or explode into a gorefest worthy of a horror movie. Instead, the monster jerked suddenly to the side, sending me crashing into the railing. I gripped on to the sword for dear life as the Leviathan's head reared back, hoisting me into the air eight feet above the deck or more.

"Ash, just do something!" I shouted, squeezing my eyes shut as sparks fanned from the sword's edge, sizzling out on my life vest. The blade had to be buried a good ten inches into the creature's neck, so why weren't the flames affecting it?

The Leviathan writhed, its head twisting toward me. It snapped at my stomach and caught a mouthful of my life vest instead. The garment deflated in an instant.

Before the Leviathan could try to take a bite out of me a second time, I lost my grip on the sword. With a wild cry, I plummeted. The sky whirled overhead, and then I slammed into the deck hard enough to knock the breath from my lungs.

At the other end of the boat, Sandra struggled to reload the harpoon gun. Drawn like a moth to a bug lamp, the Leviathan devoted its full attention to me, snapping at me in viper-quick lunges. I rolled out of the way, flinching as its teeth sank around the railing, taking out a chunk of it in the process. If the Leviathan could do that to an inch-thick metal bar, I hated to think what it would do to my arm.

As the beast coiled back, preparing for another strike, a soda can struck it in the jaw, followed by a small tackle box.

"Over here!" Naomi shouted, and the Leviathan's head swiveled toward her. No, no, no. Now wasn't the time for her to play the hero!

"R-run, Naomi," I croaked as I rolled onto my stomach, still hacking for breath.

The Leviathan reared at her, its jaws widening until I could see the spine-lined crevice of its throat. Just as it reached Naomi, a flurry of black feathers split through the air and Ash seized hold of the sword still embedded in the monster's throat. With the same brutal strength he had used to drop-kick the Behemoth, he wrenched the sword upward in a graceful flourish, beheading the Leviathan almost as effortlessly as he had decapitated my limited-edition Frankenstein action figure.

27

A NOXIOUS-SMELLING BLACK mess spewed across the deck, and the Leviathan's head crashed down with enough force to splinter the wood.

"Yeah!" Sandra pumped her fist in the air as the Leviathan's writhing body sank into the sea.

"Ash, I take back what I said about you being weak," I said, staggering to my feet. Naomi rushed to my side, her fingers tugging at my shirt.

"Are you okay, Zach?" she blubbered, and I managed a small smile and ruffled her hair.

"I'm fine, Naomi. Thanks for saving me."

Breathing heavily, Ash landed on the deck and dropped the sword. Wisps of smoke trailed up his arms, and before he curled his fingers inward, I caught a glimpse of angry red burns spreading across his palms.

"Ash, your hands…" I tentatively stepped forward. "You're hurt."

"Don't concern yourself with my welfare, human," he said aloofly, furling his wings. "As I have told you before, I am no ordinary sheyd."

Hesitantly, I touched the sword's handle. It was only slightly warm, the kind of soothing heat that reminded me of drinking hot cocoa. As I picked it up, Ash's expression hardened.

"Looks like it's not over yet," he murmured.

Swallowing hard, I followed his gaze to the severed Leviathan head at the other end of the boat. Raindrops evaporated the moment they touched the smoldering remains. The scaly skin began to crack and burn away, just as the Behemoth had disintegrated into chunks of charred flesh. Only this time, the Leviathan's neck and jaws twitched as it burned, and to my horror, it suddenly occurred to me that there was something *in* there. Something beneath its spines and scales.

"The Behemoth's core of power was in its stomach," Ash said. "When you drove the blade in, it was ruptured in an instant, before it had a chance to transform. This will be a bit harder now."

I gulped. I had played enough video games to know that the boss form was even scarier in phase two.

Slowly, a form rose from the mound of smoking meat and bone. If it was a human, its entire body was covered in a spiny exoskeleton, spikes emerging from its shoulders like a knight's pauldrons. The head was concealed beneath its own horned shell-like armor, bright gold eyes gleaming through the narrow grate of cartilage that helmeted it. A third eye opened in the center of its forehead, the place where the anglerfish-like stalk had been on the Leviathan's original form. My stomach did a flip-flop. This was a demon in all its terrible glory. This was what Ash truly was, or what he could become.

As Naomi ran behind me, the Leviathan regarded us, pale teeth gleaming through the grate of its helmet. If it could build armor from its own bone and scales, I hated to think what else it was capable of.

"It's been a few thousand years, hasn't it?" the Leviathan said in a voice as soft and hissing as rain on hot blacktop. It bared its fangs in a grin. "When did you become such a pip-squeak, Ashmedai? I almost didn't recognize you."

"It's a long story," Ash said, not smiling. A lightning bolt split across the sky, illuminating his tawny eyes, which glowed brighter with each passing moment. His nails lengthened into claws.

"It is fitting for you, brother. Tell me, since when did you start working with humans?"

"Ever since a meddlesome king enlisted me to build his temple," Ash said, and the Leviathan laughed.

"Ah, yes, I heard about that. I suppose you answer to these children now." The demon's gaze shifted to us, and its smile only grew. "Don't fret, dear brother. I will free you of your servitude."

Reaching down, the Leviathan buried its clawed hand in the still-smoldering ruins of its original form, and from the nasty pile of gunk and scales, retrieved a pike of bone. The spear's tip terminated in a lethal point.

Not good. Not good. Thinking quickly, I snatched up the flaming sword from where Ash had dropped it and lunged at the demon with a wild cry. As I swung the sword down, the Leviathan's foot shot out, and in the blink of an eye, I found myself propelled across the deck. I slammed into the railing hard enough to make my teeth rattle. Groaning, I sank onto my butt, the sword clattering to the floorboards beside me.

"Zach!" Naomi cried, rushing to my side.

"Take this, Fish Breath," Sandra shouted, and raised the harpoon gun. During the midst of the Leviathan's transformation, she had smartly reloaded. The harpoon whizzed through the air, only for the Leviathan to catch it in one hand and crush it into a twisted lump of metal.

"I'll deal with you three later," the demon said, fixing its gaze on Ash. "For now, our king and I have some unfinished business."

"Humans, get out of here," Ash told us through gritted teeth. His face had drained of color. "However you can, go now."

"We're not leaving you!" Sandra said, fumbling with the last harpoon. If not for my breathless coughing, I would've wholeheartedly agreed with her. It wasn't like we'd be able to abandon ship anyway—to reach the bright orange inflated lifeboat, we'd have to make it past the Leviathan first.

Ash opened his mouth to respond when the Leviathan lunged forward, thrusting its bone spear toward Ash's stomach. Ash darted out of the way, folding his wings against his back to avoid a second wide swipe.

With each moment, the downpour grew heavier. Lightning bolts touched down in the ocean around us, filling the air with trails of steam and making my hair stand on end.

Still wheezing for breath, I reached for the sword. My fingers splayed across rain-drenched wood. Stupefied, I looked down. Oh god, no. Had it fallen into the water?

A flash of fire caught my eye. Naomi ran across the deck, the sword gripped tightly in both hands. The weapon was only three or four pounds, but it was practically as tall as she was, and I wouldn't have trusted her to run with a pair of scissors, much less a pair of scissors *on fire*.

"Naomi, put that thing down now!" I shouted, staggering to my feet.

The Leviathan turned toward the sound of my voice. Naomi swung the sword erratically at the demon, and with the nonchalant boredom of swatting a fly, the Leviathan shifted its spear to block her blow midswing.

The moment the two weapons clashed, sparks rained down upon the deck. Whether made of bone or something far stranger, the spear was no match for the very sword that had once been used to guard the gates of Eden. Cracks spiderwebbed up the spear, and the tip fissured in two. The Leviathan's cocky smile disappeared into a bared-tooth grimace.

"Where did you get that—" the demon began, but its words were drowned out by the enraged snarl that tore from Ash's mouth. Ash lunged forward and locked his arms around the

Leviathan's waist, his talons sinking into the demon's exoskel-
etal armor. Cracks spread up its sides.

"Pip-squeak or not, you were a fool to underestimate me!"
Ash's wings flared out, sending a powerful wind blustering
across the deck. "Now, Sandra! Aim for the head!"

A blur of silver split through the air. This time, the harpoon
met its mark.

28

THE LEVIATHAN REELED back against the railing, pressing its hands over its face. As cracks spread through its shell-like helmet, the demon released a shriek so shrill and piercing, it made even my ancestors wince in their graves.

Beneath my feet, the boat's deck trembled, and the sound of splintering wood filled my ears. Then a blinding light swamped my vision, and it was as if the entire world had gone head over heels, the floor no longer beneath my feet, the sky no longer overhead—just a tumbling whirl of light and sound and color, like I'd gotten trapped in a giant kaleidoscope. Until I hit the ocean's surface.

Dark water enveloped me in an instant. With my life vest busted, I struggled to stay afloat. Waves crashed against my head and shoulders, filling my mouth with salt water and driving me under.

Sputtering, I kicked back up to the surface and blinked the droplets from my stinging eyes.

The burst of magic had torn the boat nearly in two, scattering the water with fragments of wood and metal. As I watched in horror, the boat rolled onto its side. Waves flooded the cockpit in an instant, and in the blink of an eye, half the vessel was underwater.

"Naomi! Sandra!" I searched for them in the whirlpool, gagging and gasping for breath, my throat shrunken into a pinhole. I was Naomi's big brother. I was supposed to be the one who protected her!

Drawing in a lungful of breath, I hollered Naomi's and Sandra's names until, midword, a wave smacked me in the face. Through the screen of water droplets, I caught a glimpse of a bright orange safety raft bobbing away from me.

It was the raft that had hung on the side of the boat. Inside it, Sandra and Naomi clung on for dear life.

"Zach!" Naomi reached her hands out for me even though by then she was a good twenty feet away.

"Just wait, Zach," Sandra shouted as she struggled to unhook the paddles from the raft's sides. "Just hold on. We're coming."

But the waves pushed them back toward shore. As they drifted farther and farther away, I tried to shout Naomi's name. A wave struck me, driving me back and under. Down. Down. Down. I sank lower and lower into the watery abyss, the world blurring overhead and drifting in and out of focus. My lungs strained for breath, and I struggled against the undertow that dragged me deeper. As my vision began to blur, a dark form shifted overhead. I reached out, and just when I thought my lungs were going to burst, my fingers closed around a warm hand.

Ash drew me to the surface. Wings sodden and floating loosely over the water, he dragged me over to the boat, or at least what remained of it. Only a few scraps of the boat's deck had survived, and we clambered onto one of the floating sheets of timber. The flaming sword protruded from the wood, where it must have landed after Naomi dropped it during the Leviathan fight. The blade was too wet to ignite, but wisps of steam curled from its edge the moment I grasped on to the handle to haul myself up farther.

Exhausted, I collapsed onto my hands and knees. As I wiggled the sword free and rested it slantwise across the shelf of wood, something slowly dawned on me. "Ash, you saved me. Why would you do that?"

Ash didn't answer, but from his stare, I could tell that my question had taken him aback. He clambered all the way onto the flotsam and tried to flap his wings. The feathers were sodden, and all he managed to do was throw off a cold gust of air that cast my sopping hair over my eyes.

"What can I say?" He shrugged. "It would be a shame to let you drown before I got Solomon's ring back. Besides, what is a king without his loyal subjects?"

"Oh, don't lie." A grin spread across my face. "It's because we're friends, isn't it?"

Ash sputtered for a response. "Excuse me? F-friends?"

Before I could offend him further, a red light blinked ahead, pulsing through the pounding sheets of rain. Wiping the salt water from my eyes, I squinted. "Is that…?"

"A boat," Ash whispered.

Ash's wings dissolved from sight as the vessel neared, and the searing radiance of his eyes diminished into just a spark. The boat glided through the water, so glaringly white that it glowed like a beacon. Just as it dawned on me that it might be a mirage, a man's voice blared from a speaker: "Hey, there! Hold on, we're coming!"

My shoulders loosened in relief, and I pressed my cheek to the slick wood of the rubble we clung to. "Thank god. I thought we'd become shark food. I hope Naomi and Sandra are okay."

The boat pulled up alongside us, and a man hurled a life buoy our way. Once I grabbed onto the doughnut-shaped float, he tugged it over by its rope.

"There you go," the man said, hauling me over the railing. As I skidded across the wet floor, he grasped on to the straps of my life vest and helped me regain my balance. Once Ash joined me on the deck, the man offered us a weak smile. His blond hair was plastered to the sides of his face, the kind of too-yellow shade that you could tell had come from a bottle, and so thick that I wondered if it was fake. "You kids are lucky we happened to be passing by. What happened?"

"Our boat fell apart in the storm," I said, which was at least a little more convincing than telling him that a sea monster had wrecked it.

His gaze shifted to the sword I held. "And, uh, what's that?"

"It's our dad's," I added, thinking quickly. "He hung it in the cabin as a good-luck charm. When my, uh, brother, spotted it in the wreckage, we couldn't just let it sink. Our little sister and friend managed to get into the life raft, but by the time we made it out of the boat, it was too late. Did you see them?"

"No, but we'll put out a search for them once we get back to shore. Just sit back and relax." The man wore a tan sports coat and khaki pants, both now soaked from helping us aboard. He held out his hand to me. "But first, you should probably give me that sword to hold on to. I know it's a good-luck charm, but it's not safe for a kid like you to be holding that on a moving boat."

I handed it over reluctantly. Once the sword was stowed away safely, the woman who had been steering the boat introduced herself as Trish and her companion as Henry. She had piled her brown hair almost as high as Grandma's blond beehive and treated it with enough mousse or hairspray that the wind didn't stir a single strand. Her patent leather trench coat seemed unsuitable for a day on the open water, but what did I know?

While the man took control of the wheel, Trish retreated below deck and returned with a thermos and blankets. She handed each of us a blanket and passed me the container with a warm smile. "It's coffee. It'll give you a nice jolt."

Mom and Dad wouldn't let me drink coffee, saying the caffeine would keep me up all night, but I could really use the energy right now. I took a sip and grimaced at its rank taste and oily mouthfeel. "Seriously? People really pay five bucks to drink this?"

Ash took the flask for me and downed it in several gulps. No duh, only a demon would enjoy a drink that tasted as if it'd been spewed from the bowels of the underworld.

"Sorry, kids," she said with an unsteady laugh. "We don't have anything else for you to drink, but we'll get you fixed up with some dry clothes and hot cocoa once we get back to shore."

We coasted along the shoreline. Overhead, the storm clouds had begun to dissipate, and the rain had already let up. At least we wouldn't have to worry about being electrocuted on the open water.

"Why aren't we stopping?" I asked as we passed a marina. "There's a dock right there."

"Our dock is just a few more miles down the coastline," Henry said. "There's a police station right across the street, so it'll be quicker. Just sit tight."

As he leaned over to take the empty thermos from Ash, I caught a glimpse of gold beneath his collar. My skin prickled with a sudden unease. It had almost looked like…

A low groan from beside me stirred me from my thoughts. Ash shifted, holding his hand over his stomach. "I don't feel good."

Oh great, not another pizza incident.

"You shouldn't have chugged the coffee so fast," I said.

He didn't answer. Sinking heavily against the seat, he regarded me through half-closed lids, the supernatural glow surrounding his irises slowly darkening.

"Ash?" I grasped his shoulder. He felt shockingly cold. "Ash, are you all right? What's wrong?"

He slipped from his seat and crashed to the ground.

"Hey! Something's wrong with Ash—er, with my brother!" I shouted at Trish.

She didn't even look back at us. Humming a merry tune, she rolled the wheel to the right, sending us in the direction of a deserted marina.

"Hey, didn't you hear me? You have to stop the boat!"

Suddenly, it struck me how weird it was that she and Henry hadn't asked us where our parents were. She hadn't even grilled us about why we'd decided to take a boat ride in the middle of a storm. Almost like she already knew the reason we'd been out there in the first place.

I dropped to my knees and shook Ash's shoulder. He groaned, his eyes fluttering shut. A shadow eased across the deck, slowly condensing into a limp wing, his feathers still beaded with salt water. His nails darkened and extended into claws, and one of his sopping wet sneakers tore apart as his taloned foot kicked out in sleep. I caught a whiff of coffee on his breath and…what was that? Fish?

A shadow fell over me. I looked up. Henry stared fixatedly at Ash, his eyes wide with awe and wonder.

"Magnificent," he whispered. "To think, all this time, the king of demons has walked among us. Trish, you've got to see this."

I should've known from my encounter at the zoo—never trust anyone who *liked* dressing in khakis and polo shirts.

As Henry took a step closer, I lurched forward, scrambling across the wet deck. The storage crate. I needed to get to the storage crate and get the sword—

A hand closed around my shirt, wrenching me to a stop.

"I don't think so!" Henry said, locking me in a bear hug and dragging me back.

I shocked myself by bending forward and sinking my teeth into his arm. Ugh, he tasted like sunscreen and cologne.

"Ow, he bit me!" His grip loosened, and I managed to wiggle free of him and hit the deck running.

I got to the storage crate as Henry reached me. Throwing open the lid, I grabbed at the sword. Just as my fingertips slipped over the weapon's handle, he gave me a violent shove that sent me sprawling butt-first on the floorboards. I began to rise—then froze as he pointed the sword at my throat.

"I don't think so, kid," Henry said, still panting. As I looked up at him, what I saw made my jaw drop. All the hair on top of his head had come askew and now flapped obscenely in the wind, as one solid mat. It was...a toupee?

"Nice hair," I said, unable to help myself. Apparently even the threat of sharp and pointy weapons wasn't enough to make my mouth shut up for once. At least he hadn't figured out how to set the sword on fire.

Cheeks reddening, Henry righted his hairpiece. "You're going to regret that. How would you like to be thrown back overboard?"

"Relax, Henry," Trish called from the steering wheel. "Remember what I told you, sweetie? Take deep breaths. Deep breaths now."

Henry followed her advice, breathing in steadily for several moments before turning his attention back to me. "Throwing you overboard would be too quick. Just wait for what we have in store for you, you miserable little brat."

Yeah, I didn't like the sound of that. I scooted back until I was at Ash's side once more, just in case psychopathy was catching. Whatever Trish had slipped into the coffee left Ash out cold. His wings lay unfurled limply across the deck, and even his jeans hem had begun to unravel into the original silk and embroidery.

Minutes later, we pulled up alongside a lone dock, where three men in polos and khaki pants were waiting for us. Despite their dorky uniforms, they scared the crap out of me even more than Henry and Trish. With their dark sunglasses and shaved heads, they looked like they ate nails for breakfast, along with a healthy dose of cattle steroids.

Once the boat's side was nestled securely against the dock, I jumped down and tried to barrel past the men. I hated to bail on Ash, but if I got away now, I could get help.

In a single fluid motion, one of the men grabbed me around the waist and wrenched me back. He swore as my flailing feet caught him in the shin. I tried to aim for someplace more sensitive, but instead only managed to glance my heel off his thigh. As he held me tight, another of the troll trio contorted my arms behind my back and cinched zip ties around my wrists.

"You are all making a terrible mistake," I shouted. "You will destroy the world, for what? For what?"

"Muzzle him, please," Trish said cheerfully, and the henchmen were more than happy to oblige.

Trussed like a Thanksgiving turkey, I struggled as one of the henchmen slung me over his shoulder. Except for the Knights of the Apocalypse, there wasn't a single person in sight. The dock led to a stretch of empty scrubland and a parking lot, the air muddled with the smells of coast lilac and exhaust fumes.

A black minivan was the only car in the parking lot. Unceremoniously, they threw me in the back. I rolled around on the rubber mat, struggling to sit up.

"Best settle in," Trish said with a nasty grin. "It'll be a long ride."

As she slammed the door shut, a heavy lump formed in my throat. I might never see my mom and dad after this, and what about Naomi? Someone must've rescued her and Sandra by now, right?

I hadn't even had a chance to say goodbye to them.

Moisture blurred my vision. I blinked rapidly, biting my inner cheek so that our captors wouldn't have the satisfaction of hearing me sob. Who knows, they might consider children's tears as an even greater delicacy than caviar.

As the van pulled forward, I tested the zip ties around my wrist, straining until the bands nipped into my skin. Why was something made of plastic so powerful? Couldn't they have invested in the budget zip-ties from Kidnappers R Us?

I tried to spit out the gag and grimaced. It tasted like moldy gym socks stewed in dumpster juice, and the duct tape that held the rag in place made my cheeks itch.

There had to be something I could do. There just had to.

29

AFTER WHAT FELT like an eternity, the van slowed to a stop and the door squeaked open. One of the trolls hauled me from the vehicle, swearing as I kicked his knee again.

"Would you stop that?!" he growled, as if I was the evil one here.

I wished he'd remove the nasty gym sock and duct tape they'd used as a gag. I had spent the entire ride imagining what I would say to them the moment they gave me a chance to speak. Instead, the man simply slung me over his shoulder and began walking.

I had no idea where we were, but I had no doubt it was an evil lair the likes of which only a mad scientist could dream up. Most likely, there was even an altar to sacrifice children to their Lord Cthulhu.

The man dropped me moments later. I groaned as I hit the ground and writhed into a sitting position. As I waited for my vision to adjust to the glow of the setting sun, I took in the scent of damp soil and the soft whistle of the wind through the trees.

My breath caught in my throat. I must've fallen asleep on the ride. We had gone far, much farther than I thought. We were in the redwoods—definitely not as far north as the National Forest, but maybe Butano State Park or a privately owned reserve.

And we were surrounded.

The Knights of the Apocalypse stood around me in a half circle. Aside from their matching gold medallions, none of the members were dressed in anything special. They wore the same white polo with the sewed-on badge, along with jeans, khakis, and the occasional skirt. Everyone looked like they had wandered off the set of a Disney sitcom, all freshly scrubbed faces and shiny eyes, their hair and makeup done in preparation for the end of the world.

I gawked in disbelief. Talk about terrible fashion sense. Where were the black robes? The face paint? The funny hats? I was going to be killed by a bunch of demon worshippers, and they couldn't even dress the part!

The creepy thing was that the longer I stared at them, the more difficult it was to tell them all apart. Their Hollywood-perfect faces and straight bleached smiles were so identical that I had a feeling they'd been made in test tubes and born in Dr. Frankenstein's vats. And their faces had been treated with so much Botox, their features were seamless and slightly puffy, like masks of flesh.

"Well, hello again," said the brown-haired man who'd pushed

me into the lion pit. He emerged from the crowd and squatted next to me, tearing the duct tape from over my mouth. I spit out the rag, wishing I had the confidence to spit it in his face.

Beside me, Ash lay unconscious, his wings sagging across the dirt. His modern disguise had fully disintegrated into folds of black silk and the jeweled belt he'd worn when he first appeared, but something was different now. The hem of his robe had unwound and become feathers. It dawned on me that, like the Leviathan's armor, these clothes were just another illusion of humanity. And his body was too.

"You've been a real thorn in my side, you know that?" The man poked me gently in the forehead. "A real thorn, kiddo."

"Which accursed toothpaste ad did you crawl out of?" I asked the ringleader as he flashed me a sparkling-white grin.

"Excuse me?" His smile remained, but mildly confused now, and his green eyes lost a little of their merry twinkle.

"It was Colgate, wasn't it?"

Making fun of him was almost as idiotic as calling the king of demons well-preserved, but what could I say? I had always been terrible at introductions.

The man's eyes studied me, now as flat and cold as jade disks. "You're afraid."

"No."

"You're shaking."

My mouth trembled. I didn't answer.

"This is not the end, kiddo." His smile returned. "This is only the beginning."

"Why are you even doing this? I don't get it." My voice left me in a thin croak. "What are you hoping to gain by starting the apocalypse?"

"It's not *what* that is the question. It's *where*." His gaze pierced into me, without emotion, while his smile only grew. "Eden. Once the three beasts walk the earth, once the antichrist is summoned, the gates to the Garden of Eden will be opened once more. Imagine it. A pristine paradise, untouched by all these messy issues you see in the world today. Somewhere without pain, without hunger. We will eat from the trees of life and knowledge and become immortal, our bodies preserved in this moment, as our perfect selves. And while we are there in our sanctuary, the rest of the world can just burn. Then once the dust settles, we can build society up again, in *our* image."

"Can you tell me about the aliens next?" I croaked, struggling to regain my courage.

Three perfect creases formed in his forehead as his Botox-enriched features struggled to compute his confusion. "I beg your pardon?"

"You know, the aliens. The ones who beamed you into their ship." My voice clicked, reminding me of how dry my throat felt and how hard it was to get each word out. "Because you're talking like someone who went through an alien lobotomy."

"You know, you're such a little—" He took a deep breath, his lips straining in an inflexible smile. "Well, aren't you just precious?"

"Well, aren't *you* just precious?" I mimicked back, since apparently when I'd been born, God had forgotten to give me a filter, along with a healthy dose of common sense.

The creases in his taut forehead smoothed out, and he upped the brightness of his smile by a few extra kilowatts, showing plenty of teeth and pink gumline. There was something eerie about the way his features flexed, moving along invisible creases and tendons, as if his Hollywood-handsome face was just a mask over something so grotesque it would make even Frankenstein cringe.

"You know what, on second thought, I don't think you'll live long enough to see the Garden of Eden," he said. "I could have given you this opportunity, but you're really just a simple, foolish, substandard twerp. You can just die with all the rest."

Yeah, I didn't like the sound of that at all. Why couldn't I ever seem to keep my mouth shut?

"I don't want to be invited to your apocalypse party either," I said, challenging his gaze. "I'll give you guys ten months in Eden before you start eating each other."

He laughed. "Precious."

Beside me, Ash stirred. As he groaned, his lips curled back from his teeth. His fangs were as sharp as before, sharp enough that they had punctured his lower lip in his sleep, and a thin thread of blood unraveled down his chin. When he opened his eyes, they radiated a faint and unnatural light.

His gaze met mine, and an uncontrollable shiver passed through me, a tremor so violent that my teeth chattered. I began to feel incredibly small and queasy, the way I'd felt when I visited LA's Natural History Museum for the first time and had been staggered by the incredible height of the T. rex skeleton in the Dinosaur Hall.

That was the first time I had realized how old the ground beneath me truly was, and how my existence was only a small blip in that endless reality. But this boy—this creature, this *demon*—sprawled beside me was even older and stranger than the dinosaurs that had walked the prehistoric earth millions of years before. The glow radiating from his eyes revealed that beneath his smooth features, there was something inhuman and unknowable.

"Ah, you're awake," the ringleader said, squatting down to get a better look at him. He used the bubbly singsong voice of a camp counselor. "It is so good to finally meet you. Which name do you prefer to go by? Ashmedai or Asmodeus, or perhaps Shidonai or Ashema Deva? You have so many of them."

"None of my names deserve to pass your lips, you filthy wretch," Ash snarled. "It's Your Highness for you!"

He tried to rise, only for his movements to be cut short by the chains around his ankles. He yanked at one, then winced and drew his hand against his side, but not before I caught a glimpse of the livid burn scalding his palm.

"I wouldn't try that again," the man said. "Those chains are engraved with the ineffable names of God. Just a precaution. I'm sure that you can respect that."

Warily, Ash settled onto his haunches. His gaze flicked over to me and back to the man, and he bared his teeth the way an animal would, or a demon. "Remove them this instant, human."

"I'm afraid I can't do that, Your Highness," the man said cheerfully. "However, do realize that I have great respect for you and your power, despite your…well, unexpected appearance. In fact, I admire you. Your capacity for destruction. It's like, gee, it's like being in the presence of an atomic bomb. A kid-sized one, true, but still an atomic bomb."

"Your plan won't work," I said, dismayed by the way my voice faltered. "We've already defeated the Leviathan and the Behemoth."

"Yes, you were quite a nuisance." He chuckled. "But don't worry. You see, the order of the summoning is irrelevant, only that all three beasts must walk the earth at the same time. Those siblings are the harbingers of ruin, and once they're united at last, the gateway to Eden will open for us."

I gulped. Oh crap, it was worse than I thought. He was nuttier than a squirrel convention.

"But first, this moment deserves to be commemorated," the man said, and gestured to a henchman, who came forward with an ancient Polaroid camera.

"Are you kidding me? Are you really going to take a—"

"Gather around, everyone," he called to the others. They shifted and shuffled into place, tightening their half circle around us. Once everyone was in position, he stepped in front of the crowd to take a selfie, because apparently documenting his role in the apocalypse would totally go viral. I groaned.

"Ash, do something," I whispered.

"What am I supposed to do?" he asked back.

"I don't know, but you're the king of demons. Can't you summon a demon army?"

"Oh yes, because that will make the situation so much better," he snarled.

"Come on," I pressured Ash. "Threaten to eat his soul or drag him down to hell. At the very least, pull an *Exorcist* and projectile vomit on him. Please. Anything!"

"I can't."

"There has to be something we can do to stop the Ziz from appearing."

"Zach…" A shadow passed over Ash's face, and all of a sudden, it dawned on me how regretful he looked. His gaze welled with sorrow. "It's far too late for that. I was hoping we could retrieve the ring before it came to this, but the truth is—"

"Would you two quit conspiring?" the ringleader said in aggravation, spinning around to face us. "Seriously. You're killing the mood here."

"Sorry to rain on your apocalypse party," I snapped. "But I'm not dead just yet."

"No, that will happen in—" the man glanced at his watch "—five minutes, I wager."

I swallowed hard, heart pounding against my rib cage.

Don't cry, I told myself. *Don't you dare cry.*

"But don't worry, you won't die on your knees." He smiled, gesturing to one of the members behind me. "We'll let you put up a fight. Cut the zip ties."

There was the soft *snick* of metal against plastic, and then the zip ties loosened from around my wrists. I rubbed my sore wrists, looking at the sword in the ringleader's hand. If I could just grab it…

Once he handed over the Polaroid and the fistfuls of freshly developed photos to his assistant, a woman stepped forward

222

carrying a silver tray. They had splurged on a fancy golden ring box too. The others fell silent as the man slipped the ring onto his finger. In the sunlight, the garnets encircling the signet glistened like droplets of fresh blood.

"Legend has long suggested that the three chaos beasts are singular creatures," the man said flamboyantly, as if he was giving a presidential address. "However, our founder believed that the beasts were, in fact, kings of hell, with the Behemoth being Beelzebub and the Leviathan identified as the same demon as its namesake. As for the Ziz, he is none other than Asmodeus, the king of hell whose wings were so great, that he was able to cast Solomon four hundred miles in one single draft of them. Asmodeus, the sole demon known capable of ascending to heaven to take part in celestial learning."

I gulped. No way.

The man pointed at Ash. "By the power of this ring and the cuff upon your wrist, I compel you to appear before me in your true form. Appear and wreak chaos."

3 0

BESIDE ME, ASH curled over himself and screamed—a wild and agonizing shriek that rose into an animalistic wail.

"Ash!" I reached out for him as he writhed upon the ground. There was nothing I could do, but I had to try something. I had to bring him back.

As my fingers closed around the golden bracelet Ash wore around his wrist, a searing light filled my vision. Before I knew it, I felt my body being hurled through space and time, everything reduced to a bright frantic smear of color and movement, until all that remained was his anguished roar scraping against my eardrums until I thought they'd burst.

Driven back, back, back—until I found myself standing before Solomon once more, only now he lay upon a stately gilded bed in a smaller chamber, his face buried in wrinkles and greasy with sweat. As his dark eyes fixed at me, he drew in a laborious breath and released it slowly, in evident pain. He beckoned.

"Come closer, demon," he croaked, baring his teeth in a joyless smile. "Have you come to watch the proud king fall? Or do you intend to replace me once more?"

"I came merely to observe your passing," a smooth voice said, low and ageless. It was not a human voice—just a soft, flowing noise that made me think of the lapping of the ocean waves against a rocky northern shore, or the hiss of the wind passing through redwoods, the sounds of nature taking on a human form.

"Of course you have. You've always enjoyed a good show."

"I heard word of your inevitable passing within the celestial study halls," Ash said, and I found my own lips shaping around the words, words I had never spoken, in a language I did not understand and yet I knew perfectly, as though it were a part of my blood. "You disappoint me, Solomon. I was expecting something with a bit more flair, but here you are, gasping like a beached fish upon the shore. My, how the mighty have fallen, milord."

"Yes, I'm afraid that unlike you, we humans age and die. But what does a hundred years mean to you? What does each day mean to you? An hour? A mere minute with the people closest to you? It is because of our short life spans that we humans can appreciate every moment and that we are capable of love. Can you say the same, demon?"

"To be fair, I'm actually getting a lot of enjoyment from this moment," Ash said, drawing closer. "Would you like me to end your pain? I can make it go silently, gently. A last kindness, if you will."

"No, but I do have one last request of you," Solomon said. "Change yourself into something more soothing. I don't wish to die with your ugly face seared in my memory."

Ash laughed. "As you wish, milord."

A breeze passed through the chamber, stirring the linen curtains draped over the bed.

"Would you prefer Naamah?" Ash asked, and his voice grew softer, into a woman's murmur. Cast across the wall in the flickering candlelight, I caught a glimpse of a skeletal shadow, a bold skull and arched rib cage draped in gauzy silk.

Solomon closed his eyes, and even though he laughed—a strange, painful sound—tears glistened down his cheeks. "You are truly a profane beast."

"She was your wife," Ash said, and the silhouette of feathered wings swept across the limestone columns. Not just a single pair, but many. "Do you not wish to see her again?"

"You come before me as she is now, not as she was. Show me something else. Show me my son when he was but a child."

"If you insist," Ash said, his voice softening into the way it was now. He stepped deeper into the chamber and in the bronze mirror hanging on the wall, I caught a glimpse of him—dark haired and bronze skinned, his golden eyes dulling to a gentle shade of amber.

"Is this better?" he asked, his lips rising in a smile.

"Perfect," Solomon said. "Now. Would you come closer? Sit by my side. Talk to me."

"What shall I tell you about, old man? Do you wish to hear who will be born today and who will die? Or do you yearn to hear about the squabbles and debates of the celestial study halls? I'm afraid all information I can give you is useless. We don't have much time left. By the time they light the evening candles, you will be gone, milord. By tomorrow, you will find your place beneath the earth, like all the kings who have come before you, and as you are lost to the dust, I will continue on."

"You say it as though you are pleased," Solomon said quietly. "So, why are you crying?"

I could feel the sharp sting of tears overflowing my eyes and taste their salt upon my lips. Beneath Ash's cruel words, he felt no satisfaction, just grief like a cutting blade.

"You can tell me a story," Solomon said. "Tell me about how you allowed yourself to be bested by little more than a keg of wine and a bundle of wool. You, the king of all demons. You arrogant fool."

Before Ash could answer, Solomon's hand darted out from under the covers and seized hold of Ash's wrist. I caught a glimpse of gold between the man's fingers, felt cold metal cinch around my wrist. There was the soft *click* of a lock falling into place. When Ash pulled away, Solomon left a gold cuff studded with garnets and inscribed in Hebrew.

"My bequeathal to you," Solomon said with a bitter smile. "To replace the anklet you lost. You'll find that it works just as effectively in binding my will to you."

Ash's voice rose in outrage. "How dare you—"

"My last command, king of demons, is that you stay within this form, this weak and human form, and for the first time in your cursed existence, understand what it is to feel fear and powerlessness in this world. To understand the terror of a child stumbling through the dark."

"What have you done?!"

"Although I enjoyed the thought of you shambling around as a skeleton, I would not disgrace Naamah's memory. And I think that for a creature as immature and petulant as you, this form will be a bit more befitting. Go live a long life, Ashmedai."

31

I OPENED MY EYES, wincing at the glow of the setting sun. My body ached, and twigs and dead leaves crunched beneath me as I rolled over onto my stomach. I'd been thrown ten feet, but I didn't think I'd broken only bones, only gotten bruises.

Sawdust and dirt clouded the air. Groaning, I hoisted myself into a sitting position, looking around at the Knights' awed faces. It took me a moment to recognize what they were staring at, as a massive shape prowled from the haze.

The Ziz.

It, no, *he* stared at me, unwavering. I had expected something like a giant bird, but the creature that confronted me was more griffin than raptor, his huge golden eyes peered down at me from a broad, angular face, the face of a lion. Glossy black feathers engulfed him from head to toe, the pinions long enough that when the wind ruffled them, they almost resembled fur.

Ash had called his true form magnificent, and it was, but he had conveniently omitted the fact that it was also utterly *ter-rifying*. Ram horns twisted from his brow, and the teeth that were exposed when he peeled back his black lips were deadly sharp. Feathered wings curled against his sides.

My mouth trembled.

"Ash," I croaked, but there was no recognition in the beast's gaze. There was nothing but a cruel, inhuman stare, almost reptilian in its coldness.

Where was a barrel full of fish when we needed it? It dawned on me that Sandra and I never should've gotten involved in this mess alone. At the very least, we should have recruited the sub place where Carmen acquired her unholy tuna melts.

"Majestic," the ringleader said, stepping forward. His green eyes shone with awe. "He is even greater than I imagined."

He reached out a hand, like Ash was a giant kitten eager for ear rubs. There was a blur of black feathers and flared wings, and the man was launched across the clearing by a single swipe of Ash's paw.

Clamoring voices rose around me, and the amazement in the crowd's eyes quickly dimmed into terror. They stumbled back as Ash lunged forward, and I rolled out of the way to avoid being trampled beneath his giant bird feet.

In the corner of my eye, the glow of the setting sun danced across a shard of honed steel. I turned.

The sword had been flung across the clearing by the force of Ash's transformation and gotten embedded in a tree trunk about fifteen feet above ground. I had to reach it. As I made a dash for the sword, Ash roared.

His heavy tread crunched through the soil behind me, paws striking the earth as loudly as cannon blasts. The knights scattered, darting for cover. Someone screamed, and then went silent, and I tried to block out the noise, because this wasn't a movie; this was real and there was actually someone hurt back there.

As I reached the tree where the sword was, the sudden beat of paw strikes sounded from behind me, and I turned just in time to see Ash lunging toward me like a cat chasing a mouse. I ducked behind the tree. His teeth snapped the air where I had been moments before, taking out a huge chunk of the trunk in the process.

"Ash, snap out of it!" I shouted, but he only flung himself against the trunk so violently that the branches shuddered, and a crack raced up the tree. Leaves rained down, followed by the sharp *whizz* of an object falling through the air. The flaming sword drove into the ground, blazing from tip to hilt.

I darted forward and seized the sword, though I wasn't sure how much good it would do to fight from the ground when Ash's head was so high up. If I stabbed him in the paw, it would probably feel no worse than stepping on a Lego, which all things considered, was pretty painful.

Ash slammed against the trunk once more, and I ran, praying to find a shelter that would actually withstand a few good strikes. There had to be something I could do. There had to be a way to stop this.

A shadow passed over me, and I looked up as Ash descended in a death swoop, his talons unsheathed. Seriously? Compared to the Knights of the Apocalypse, I'd barely be an appetizer! Not to mention those people had probably grown up on diets of caviar and steak. They would be far tastier.

"Stop this, Ash!" I shouted as I ran. "I'm begging you. I know you don't want to do this."

Ash landed, and I twisted around to confront him. He crouched twenty feet away, a distance he would be able to bridge easily. His powerful muscles flexed beneath his sleek black feathers.

"Ashmedai." Panting, I gazed into his searing golden eyes. The pupils were slit like a cat's and flared at the sight of me. "I know you're in there. And I know you are hurting. I saw your memories. What King Solomon did to you was wrong! He never should've tricked you like that. He never should have made you build the temple, when it wasn't something you wanted to do!"

His muzzle wrinkled, nostrils flaring. He bared his teeth at me, a low warning growl rising from deep within him.

"Please, just listen to me. I know you're a demon, but you're also my friend." I spoke rapidly, praying to draw him back somehow. "And I know there's good in you."

He stepped forward, covering eight feet in an instant, and my gaze landed on his birdlike paws, scaled and tipped with lethal talons. A glint of gold caught my eye, drawing my gaze to the cuff encircling his front paw. Compared to the shackles that the Knights of the Apocalypse had fitted him with, his ancient garnet-studded bracelet had managed to not just survive the transformation, but *adapt* to it, no doubt imbued with a magic of its own.

An idea flashed in my head like a light bulb. Twisting around, I broke into a dead sprint.

No doubt determined to have one final snack before he started the apocalypse, Ash hunted me relentlessly, pouncing between trees and digging up great clouds of soil and broken roots in his wake. He took to the sky with a deafening roar that caused the trees to quake, raining leaves all around us.

Terrified to look up, I forced myself to keep running, searching for a tree that would work for my plan.

Ahead, I spotted a fallen redwood whose trunk had gotten trapped in the V-shaped crook of another tree that was still standing. The two trees created a triangular gap high above ground. Perfect.

I raced toward the tree with Ash in ruthless pursuit. As I made it through the opening, Ash barreled at me. He was too tall to make it through the gap, and swatted at me with one paw, claws extended and teeth bared. I ducked away, mere inches from being crushed beneath his talons.

His paw came down with a crash, sending dirt and pebbles spewing between the trees. Praying I wouldn't regret this, I lunged forward and clambered up his outstretched claw, grabbing fistfuls of feathers to haul myself farther up, until I reached the cuff.

"I'm sorry, Ash!" I slammed the sword into the golden band and was rewarded with an outpouring of sparks. A crack formed down the center of the cuff. I brought the sword down once more, driving it even farther into the crevice.

A roar of rage or anguish tore from Ash's throat, and with a single flap of his massive wings, he took to the sky. Gripping on to his feathers and the leathery hide beneath, I pressed myself against the cuff as the ground shrunk to a green blur beneath us.

My grip faltered on the sword, and it nearly slipped from my sweaty fingers. I tightened my hold, trying to convince myself to yank it free. But we were even higher now and wrenching the blade from the crack might make me lose my balance. I didn't have to look back to know it was a long way down.

Sparks poured from the edge of the blade as I wiggled the blade back and forth. I freed it at last, holding my breath as I brought the blade down with all my strength.

The third time was the charm. As the crack spread from the top of the cuff to the bottom, my vision was immersed in a blinding light, and I was flung from Ash's claw with sickening force.

I fell, plummeting head over heels. The redwood forest stretched below in a dizzying green carpet. I opened my mouth to scream, but no words came out. My breath seized in my lungs, the air thinner here and ice-cold. So cold.

The redwood trees rose up to greet me. In the ruby sunlight, their branches appeared as sharp as blades.

I never felt myself hit the ground.

32

JUST BEFORE I broke through the canopy, taloned hands closed around my rib cage. Black feathered wings curled around me like a pair of cupped palms, shielding my view of the earth that was rapidly approaching. As I screamed, preparing for impact, the wings unfurled to catch the wind, slowing our fall to a smooth descent.

My legs gave out beneath me as we touched down on the forest floor. I sank to my knees, trembling.

All I could make of Ash was the ebony sprawl of his wings curtaining me on either side, and I began to lift my head, but it was like my spine had locked in place. I was afraid to look at him directly, sensing deep down that the moment the cuff had shattered, so had his illusion of humanity. If I looked him in the eye, I felt—no, I *knew* it would be like staring at the sun for too long. It might blind me outright.

"Not yet," Ash said as if sensing my thoughts. His voice came out quiet and flowing, like the wind through leaves. It was the voice of the demon who had visited King Solomon's deathbed. "In the darkness, I heard someone call my name. It was you, Zach, wasn't it? You brought me back."

"Of course I did." I swallowed hard, trying to steady my voice. "What are friends for?"

"Indeed." He chuckled, and this time he sounded a little more like himself. "But best not look just yet. I'm afraid the truth can be quite terrifying."

Figures emerged from the haze of dust created by Ash's chase—men and women whose perfectly coiffed haircuts were now ruined and windblown. Dirt covered their dorky uniforms and blank faces.

The ringleader staggered forward, his face dead white except for a garish smear of blood down his cheek. He stared intently at me. "Wh-what have you done, you fool? You ruined it all. All of it."

"Did you think I was your trained dog?" Ash asked in a soft, deadly voice from behind me. "Something that you could control? Oh, how foolish you are. How arrogant…"

The man's face grew even paler. He thrust out a hand, pointing his ringed finger at Ash. "I am commanding you to stop—"

"Your commands are empty words, as the ring no longer holds any power over me. My siblings were weak and easy for you to sway, but I am not so. And unlike them, I do not need to be awakened, for I am already awake."

Ash stayed out of sight, but I could hear the smile in his voice. I gulped. This was about to get ugly.

The ringleader sank to his knees, and with looks of fear and bafflement, the others followed. He pressed his quivering hands together. "Please, understand that I have a great respect for you."

"Don't patronize me."

"P-please, have mercy and spare us."

"Oh, I don't plan to kill you. No, not at all. In fact, I'm going to give you exactly what you want." Ash chuckled. "You want to go to the Garden of Eden? I will take you there, gladly. But I suspect you will find it has changed greatly in the years since Adam and Eve."

A powerful wind blustered against my back, accompanied by the rustling of what sounded like not just one set of wings but *many*.

The trees quivered. Beneath my feet, the ground trembled, as if the gust was strong enough to peel back the packed soil in a single sheet. Talons curled around my shoulders.

In the corner of my eye, I caught a glimpse of gold eyes, clawed hands stippled black with pinfeathers, and a silk shroud that had partially tattered into yet more feathers. From the glance alone, I began to tremble.

"Close your eyes," Ash said, "and fear nothing."

Growing even stronger, the howling wind stripped the leaves from the trees and brewed up a tornado of dirt. The air was filled with the sound of a thousand wings. I squeezed my eyes shut as the squall rushed over me. From beyond the darkness came voices—cries, screams, a single enraged shout.

"I will make you pay for this," the ringleader howled. "Both of you."

And then it was silent. The wind died down in an instant, and the stillness settled over me like a curtain. I opened my eyes and gaped. All trees within a thirty-foot radius were gone, just gone, with craters where their roots had once been. And the Knights of the Apocalypse were nowhere to be found.

The talons curled around my shoulders became human fingers.

"Ash, what did you…?" I trailed off.

"I did what I promised."

Ash stepped past me, and he was as he had been—just a boy wearing a dark, flowing tunic, crown, and jeweled belt, a boy with wings furled against his back and a raven's clawed feet.

He leaned down and picked up Solomon's ring, regarding it thoughtfully. "Strange, how such a tiny thing could have so much power, isn't it? It was given to Solomon by the archangel Michael, do you know that? Angels always trying to meddle in things."

"So, it's over then?" I asked.

He nodded. "It's over. For now."

I looked at the sky. The sun was sinking by the minute. My parents were probably freaking out right now. I had no doubt that when I returned, they'd ground me for months.

"How are we going to get back?" I asked.

238

A sly smile spread across his lips. "I have an idea."

"I don't like the sound of that."

"Prepare yourself, human. As thanks, I will take you on a night flight."

33

LIKE A COMET, we hurtled through the dusky sky. Wind scraped at my face, pushed my hair out of my eyes. Keeping a steady grip on my rib cage, Ash flew so fast that gravity seemed to lose its hold over us, so that even when I kicked out my legs to steady myself, it was like the air formed a dense cushion beneath me. I almost believed that if he let go of me, I wouldn't fall but rise even higher.

Down below, rolling hills replaced the towering redwoods. To the west, the sun gleamed darkly against the ocean, transforming it into a gilded banner crested with magenta and crimson.

I had always been a little afraid of heights, but something changed this time. From this high up, it was impossible to tell how far we were above ground. And even as Ash coasted higher until we reached the low-hanging clouds, his grip remained steadfast. We surged through the misty cloud layer, and I shocked myself by laughing, then hollering like I was on the corkscrew twist of a roller-coaster ride, spreading out my arms.

We returned to a lower altitude and coasted along smoothly. Car lights winked along the branched roads and highways.

"What about the flaming sword?" I asked, once I managed to gather in enough air to speak. "Could it still be down there?"

"Undoubtedly so. It would take more than that to destroy an object imbued with divine will."

"Are you going to take the ring and sword with you?"

"Better that they stay on earth," Ash said. "They'd find their way back eventually. But don't worry, I'll find a safe place for them, with someone who knows how powerful they are and how important it is to protect them."

"Who?"

"Oh, I have a few people in mind." I could hear the smirk in his voice.

As we followed the coastline, the sky deepened to indigo, and the sun sank below the horizon. Stars surfaced from the night like a scatter of diamonds, and a crescent moon dipped through the clouds.

We touched down on an expanse of white sand flanking luxury condos. My legs collapsed beneath me the moment we landed, as if they'd forgotten how to walk on solid ground, and I laughed until I could barely catch my breath.

As I rose to my feet, the wind whipped off the water, rustling Ash's wings. I didn't realize we weren't alone until I heard a soft gasp and turned to find a dog-walker staring slack-jawed at us. Her Dalmatian looked almost as shocked as herself.

"I c-can't believe it," she stammered. "What's going on? You two—you two just came out of the sky. And you. You have wings. Why do you have wings?!"

Ash stepped forward and offered her a smile, his wings already dissipating into darkness. "It's all right. What you see now is merely a dream."

She nodded hesitantly. "It is?"

"Just a dream," he repeated.

Her eyes glazed over. "Oh... I see."

"When you look back to this moment, you'll remember that you were on the beach and you were tired, you were so tired. You sat down and drifted off, just for a moment. Just long enough. Now, would you please let me borrow your phone?"

Just listening to his voice made me a little drowsy myself. When he handed me her phone, it took me a moment to remember Sandra's number. It dialed twice before she picked up.

"Hello?"

"Sandra, it's me." My shoulders weakened in relief. "Me and Ash, we're safe."

"Oh, thank god." She drew in a wavering breath. "Your sister is fine. We washed ashore a few miles down the coast and we're with Carmen."

"Please tell me you didn't call my parents?"

"Uh, not yet. Carmen wanted to, but I told her that you were probably fine since you had Ash and all, and how were we going to explain a stolen boat? But we called the coast guard. We're at their station now."

"Don't call my mom and dad, or they'll ground me forever. Just wait there. We'll come to you."

I hung up the phone and gave it back to the woman, who continued to stare dazedly into the distance. I wanted to ask her for a ride, but then figured it was probably better not to get in a car with someone who looked one moment away from going to la-la land.

"I'll stay with you until you reach home," Ash said as we crossed the beach. "But after that, there is something I need to do."

"Where will you go from here?" I asked.

"Who knows? I think I'll pay a visit to my friends up above. It's been a good three thousand years since I've crushed them in a debate. As for the ring, the only reason it was able to control me was because of the bracelet. I'm stronger than my siblings, the strongest among us, and now that the ring has lost its hold over me, it will never be able to compel me again." His radiant gaze shifted toward me. "I have you to thank for that, Zach."

"Now that you're free, why don't you transform back to your original form?"

"What you saw back there was my original form, or the closest thing to it. What Solomon saw, and what you see now, is a part of me, not a whole. Though I will admit, after a few thousand years, I've actually grown a bit fond of this form. It's taught me humility." He smiled wryly. "I guess that's what Solomon wanted all along."

"Will I see you again?" I asked.

"Do you want to?"

"Yeah, of course I do. We're friends after all."

"Friends," he repeated, and nodded thoughtfully, with a vague smile. "Yeah, I guess we are, aren't we?"

"Definitely."

"You know, for a demon, you're not so bad," I said as we climbed the beach toward the glow of passing headlights.

He grinned. "I could say the same about you, human."

With each step we took, he grew more and more transparent. By the time we reached the parking lot, he was a shadow, and then no more than the soft whisper of feathers against blacktop.

EPILOGUE

GROUNDED AGAIN!

No TV, no video games or computer, not even my phone this time. I groaned, flipping through my *Goosebumps* collection for about the hundredth time this weekend. Even the "choose your own adventure" stories couldn't grab my attention.

Sighing, I sprawled on my bed, retrieving the gold ouroboros pendant from the top drawer of my nightstand. I held it up to catch the sunlight, lazily tilting it back and forth until the engraved snake appeared to move. Now that the sword and ring were gone, the pendant was the only proof that Ash had ever existed, that those things had actually happened.

The window was raised, and a minifan whirred on my nightstand, but it was hot enough in my room that I'd probably be able to cook hotdogs on the windowsill. I wished I could go over to Sandra's and swim in her pool. Too bad my parents knew just how to torture me, so they'd banned me from visiting her too. It was a shock Mom and Dad hadn't been recruited by the jailers at Alcatraz by now.

The hours after Ash had landed on the beach had been total chaos. Apparently, after Naomi and Sandra had washed ashore at a private beach several miles down the coast, they had managed to find Carmen with the help of a panicking sunbather. Being the adult—er, teen—of the group, Carmen had sent the coast guard out in search of Ash and me, although not before coming up with a convincing cover story about how an undertow had carried us out from shore.

Luckily, the coast guard hadn't bought Naomi's incoherent story about a sea serpent and demon king, and Sandra had the sense to give false names and conveniently omit the fact that we had stolen a boat.

In the end, my parents never found out about the boat, let alone my near brush with death. They had grounded me for the crime of losing my phone and ignoring their calls until eleven o'clock at night, when Carmen had pulled up in front of my house in her borrowed Volkswagen to drop Naomi and me off.

It was a good thing they hadn't figured out the truth, because then I wouldn't just be grounded for a week. They'd have put me on house arrest until I was fifty!

Jeffrey didn't return to school the rest of the week. A lot of rumors flew around about his absence, especially when news broke that his dad's boat had washed ashore in pieces. Half the class believed that he had been sent to juvenile hall, the other half thought he switched schools, and the few who remained suggested he had been abducted by aliens. I was secretly hoping for the alien theory, but then our teacher had told us the true reason he was out of school, and my stomach had dropped in an instant.

His dad's boat wasn't the issue. It was his dad. The man had disappeared that same day, just drove off after getting an urgent phone call, abandoning Jeffrey and his friends at the beach. I kept telling myself it had to be a coincidence, but it still didn't keep me from feeling a twinge of guilt.

In any case, I was just glad that Jeffrey was gone for the time being. Without their President Sasquatch to guide them, the rest of his gang quickly lost interest in me and shuffled around class like a pack of lost puppies.

Even Dominic kept a wide berth, but not before coming up to me during lunch period with a guilty look on his face and apologizing for the whole beach thing. I didn't know what to make of it, only that I'd never feel the same way about him again. He had shown himself to me for who he truly was, who he had always been.

Anyway, when Jeffrey returned—*if* he returned—I had a feeling he wouldn't be bothering me from now on. Unless he figured out about the whole "yeah, my demon friend might've just hurled your dad into the Garden of Eden and all" thing.

I was stirred from my thoughts by the rustling of the window curtains. A sudden breeze passed through the room, plucking the fishline tethering my models to the ceiling until the Mothman cryptid nearly collided with the USCSS *Nostromo*.

I sat up quickly. "Ash?"

The sun glinted through the swaying drapes. Jumping to my

247

feet, I rushed to the window and peered out. The only thing to greet me was an annoyed-looking pigeon, who glowered at me from the branches of the nearby tree.

Sighing, I slid the window shut. The bottom of the pane struck an object with a metallic clang. I looked down.

A bundle wrapped in black silk rested atop the sill. Holding my breath, I unfolded the fabric. It disintegrated into feathers beneath my touch, and then to soot, until all that remained were the flaming sword and Solomon's ring, glinting like treasures from the ashes.

* * * * *

ACKNOWLEDGMENTS

THIS BOOK WAS such a blast to write! Zach's voice came to me in an instant, and I knew right away who I wanted him to be and the kind of character he was. I absolutely adored working on *The Ring of Solomon*, and all of this wouldn't have been possible without the support and encouragement of my agent, Thao Le, who asked me if I wanted to try writing a middle grade book in the first place. Thanks to her, I brainstormed the idea for the story, and to my utter delight, it evolved into what it is today.

Another person who was instrumental in this process was my editor, Stephanie Cohen, whose wonderful notes helped me bring Zach and his friends to life. With each revision, my vision for the story became clearer, and by the end of the editing process, the trio shone off the page.

Additionally, I would like to thank everyone at Inkyard Press who has made this book a reality. In particular, I would like to thank Bess Braswell, Justine Sha, and Brittany Mitchell, as well as the marketing and library outreach teams. Additionally, I would like to thank the cover artist, Arthur Bowling III, for creating such a wonderfully dynamic cover, and Jon Reyes for sensitivity reading for Latinx and queer rep.

Lastly, I'd like to thank my critique partners for helping me throughout this entire process. Your support and encouragement have been invaluable in this journey.